The Bonjour Gene

THE AMERICAS

The Bonjour Gene

A Novel

J. A. Marzán

Introduction by
David Huddle

The University of Wisconsin Press

The University of Wisconsin Press
1930 Monroe Street, 3rd Floor
Madison, Wisconsin 53711-2059
uwpress.wisc.edu

3 Henrietta Street
London WC2E 8LU, England
eurospanbookstore.com

Printed in the United States of America

Library of Congress Cataloging-in-Publication Data

Marzán, Julio, 1946–
The bonjour gene / by J. A. Marzán.
p.   cm.—(The Americas)
ISBN 0-299-20410-3 (hardcover: alk. paper)
I. Title.   II. Americas (Madison, Wis.)
PS3563.A768B66   2005
813'.54—dc22   2004012827

ISBN 978-0-299-20414-3 (pbk.: alk. paper)
ISBN 978-0-299-20413-6 (e-book)

This book is dedicated to

CLARISSA JULIA MARZÁN
and to all descended from Mont de Marsan

Contents

Acknowledgments

Chapters of this book have previously appeared in journals or anthologies:

"Unforgettable Tangos, Indelible Pagodas" was published in the *Americas Review* and is reprinted with permission from Arte Público Press.

"Tying the Knot" was published in the *Nassau Review*.

"B-Movie" was published in *Ishmael Reed's Konch Magazine*.

"What We Should Know about the Climb to Heaven" originally appeared in the *Kenyon Review*, new series 14, no. 1 (winter 1992), with the title "What We Don't Know about the Climb to Heaven," and was reprinted in the anthology *Currents from the Dancing River: Contemporary Latino Fiction, Nonfiction, and Poetry*, edited by Ray González (New York: Harcourt Brace, 1994).

"The Bonjour Gene," under the title "The Ingredient," first appeared in the anthology *Iguana Dreams: New Latino Fiction*, edited by Delia Poey and Virgil Suarez (New York: Harper-Perennial, 1992).

Narrative Structure and Family Complication

An Introduction to J. A. Marzán's The Bonjour Gene

David Huddle

Most families are complicated, but the French-originating, Puerto Rican, USA-bound Bonjours, with their inclination to father children both in and out of wedlock, are maybe the most complicated of all. Not only do the men go beyond family in their procreational activities, they also do their best to get away from family—but then they yearn to go back. The "bloodline," as J. A. Marzán terms it, flings Bonjours out across the island of Puerto Rico and up into North America, but then it reels them back—to the fathers, to the source, to the family. Evidently there's no disowning a Bonjour; however distantly connected, whenever there's a funeral they're summoned home, they're embraced and encouraged to commune with those sharing the curse of the bloodline. The men behave badly—and they curse themselves even as they're doing it—but the women collaborate, by putting up with the reckless womanizing and even by sharing in the fascination with it. "Go see your father," a Bonjour ex-wife will say, even though she despises the father's womanizing ways.

Every immigration story is also a story about family, language, and survival. Julia Alvarez's *How the Garcia Girls Lost Their Accents* and Junot Díaz's *Drown* are intriguingly different and similar immigration narratives by Dominican American writers. Alvarez's affluent and educated Garcias carry out struggles of consciousness; Díaz's poverty-stricken de las Casases grapple with violence, drugs, and the monstrous forces of the U.S. economy. Marzán's Bonjours are so various in their fortunes that some are like the Garcias and others like the de las Casases. And it is this variety—of luck and social class and education, all within a single family—that is Marzán's singular contribution to American immigration literature. Formally known primarily for his poetry and translations, Marzán is now a novelist who has opened up some elbow room in a genre that needed a little refreshment.

Technically, however, the most notable characteristic *The Bonjour Gene* has in common with Alvarez's and Díaz's books is its hybrid structure—half novel and half "linked stories." Chaucer's *Canterbury Tales* is certainly one of the earliest manifestations of the linked-stories structure. Its North American "bloodline" flows from Washington Irving's *The Sketch Book* to Sherwood Anderson's *Winesburg, Ohio* to Ernest Hemingway's *In Our Time* to Jayne Anne Phillips's *Black Tickets* to Tim O'Brien's *The Things They Carried*. Authors who resort to this structure use it when their subject matter is so unruly that a straightforward, linear approach is out of the question. These Bonjours will submit only to a narrative method that allows them the freedom they demand but that also enforces the discipline of a detailed report. There are no happy Bonjours, but their unhappiness is infinitely various. The only way to understand the whole of the family, its history, and its future is to consider enough parts of it to get the picture.

Worthy of special attention here are Daisy Bonjour, who falls in love with a man because she loves his writing and "the sense of order she experienced in his room"; Philip Bonjour, a small boy navigating without his father, past his junkie mother's death, toward survival by way of his aptitude for computer games; and Isabel Bonjour, one of the most admirable characters one is likely to encounter in contemporary fiction. At the very center of this book is the mysterious and violent death of Edgar Bonjour. Marzán's remarkable achievement in these pages is to demonstrate the historical necessity of that death as well as the extent and subtlety of the shock waves emanating from that death. Sociologically, what brings an end to Edgar Bonjour is the explosive mix of his heritage as a Bonjour, his American social aspirations, and his sudden, intense desire to return to Puerto Rico. His mistake is in trying to undo what he has become. All the parts of this novel spring from the Bonjour bloodlines and the death of one oddly crucial member of the family. By the time we finish reading the book, however, we understand that Edgar is atypical—a throwback. Bonjours in general know how to survive their own self-destructive impulses, how to adapt and move forward.

In fact, if William Faulkner's Compsons are a doomed family that has reached its decadent conclusion, then J. A. Marzán's Bonjours are a work-eternally-in-progress. *The Bonjour Gene* shows this family to be hardy, resourceful, and adaptable. As the Compsons fade from the history of the U. S. South, the Bonjours will continue living and writing the new global history. For readers in the twenty-first century United States, *The Bonjour Gene* offers some practical advice: *Evolve!* Of course, Marzán probably intends no direct political message—but the novel he's written demonstrates the essential force that sustains this bloodline. And the novel he's written—about a family struggling with the complexity of its own heart—is a powerful global-American story.

Prologue

In the early 1800s three brothers from the south of France traveled to Cádiz, from where they sailed to Puerto Rico in pursuit of the two natural resources in which that tropically lush but Crown-forsaken island was still said to be rich: beautiful women and coffee that Rome once decreed exclusively fit for the palate of a pope. Adhering to their plan, the brothers purchased adjoining mountain lands, married beautiful women, and cultivated coffee that they exported to Europe—lucky that by their first yield shipping had improved dramatically since they arrived to discover that, unless to drop off a passenger, captains would rather bypass the misnomered Rich Port for the hub and hubbub of Havana.

But the proliferation of ships in San Juan's harbor also ironically augured a reversal of the brothers' fortune. Ships that used to sail on to Spain now did stop—but to unload loyalist exiles from rebelling colonies and to profit from Madrid's paying closer, repressive attention to its smallest American colony. For its geographic position closest to Europe, on which the brothers had counted to make their business profitable, also made this lesser island the empire's maritime gateway to be guarded—this time not from yesteryear's pirates and rival navies but from the future's liberal ideas. To cut off that poison, presumably infused by contact with other countries, all publications, including imported books, were censored, and just as stringently, all island commerce was chained to Iberian cities. Against that monopoly, the brothers' exquisite coffee fared little better than selling it to the local market, where they were forced to turn, offering as well tropical produce from the same lands where their children had already grown and were having children of their own.

By the time the Anglo-Saxon victors of the Spanish-American War unexpectedly demanded the ceding of Puerto Rico, the brothers were already in their graves. The new colonial government zoned their children's mountain lands into a single rural ward named after their ubiquitous surname, Bonjour, no longer remembered for coffee but better known for its concentration of French-descended families that reproduced rampant adulterers. For if wealth from coffee proved beyond their reach, the brothers still plundered the island's other treasure, each begetting two, and in one case three, bastard lineages that begat sons and grandsons who did the same.

And so the most enduring Bonjour inheritance was a memory of betrayals and abandonment, a legacy that to this day haunts their descendants both on the island and across the Atlantic, latitudes up in New York City, where removed families now strangers to each other remain connected by the lore of their single bloodline and the curse that every Bonjour male carries a reckless, womanizing gene.

The Bonjour Gene

B-Movie

Benjamin Martin's thoughts had drifted far from his driving on the New Jersey Turnpike until he realized that, again, he was grinding his teeth. Nervous, as if anyone could hear the grinding over the steady, wind-hummed decibels, he glanced through his sunglasses at Betty, a green-tinted cameo, her hair in a bun, who hadn't spoken since plopping into the Volvo, "Edgar doesn't deserve our seeing him buried, especially in this heat." Benjamin couldn't agree more and would have said so if he didn't believe that the real target of her anger wasn't Edgar but himself, or more precisely the image of him impressed on her by the two detectives.

They had come over the night before last. The thin one wore a plaid jacket, a crew cut and a friendly smile. The heavy-set one, in a rumpled blue suit, was prematurely silver-gray, and his blue eyes grilled the world. He was the one who telephoned that afternoon, explaining that the police already had thick files on Edgar's new friends. "But we really don't have anything on him. His arrival on that scene introduced threads we'd like to discuss with you. We believe you might have information that could help solve the murder of your best friend."

"Former best friend," Benjamin corrected him and insisted that he had no information, having been kept in the dark about Edgar's secret life. But as this accuser had a way of making a demurral stink of something held back, Benjamin agreed to have them over if only to get the matter done with that night.

The interview took place at the Martins' dining table. Crewcut held out a small notepad with a list of five names. Did Benjamin remember any? They were from his old neighborhood, names he hadn't heard in thirty years. Thinking it absurd that he should be expected to say something about names now light-years from his life, he answered flippantly, "I maybe remember two, vaguely. Is that it?" Not humored, Crewcut asked—in a tone that warned him to take this matter more seriously—if he could give any detail or description of those remembered names.

Benjamin repeated, this time soberly, that, yes, he did remember two names, but he could only describe their owners as he remembered them thirty years ago. He wouldn't know what they looked like today and probably wouldn't recognize them if they stood in front of him.

The heavy detective inquired, "Okay, let's put the list aside. Was there anything that Edgar might have said, anything confidential that would only be shared with a best friend?"

"Nothing, our friendship had been breaking down for a year."

Heavy glanced at Crewcut before following up, "Was there anything confidential Edgar might have told you before that time, when you were closer?"

Benjamin shook his head.

"No girlfriend, no sexual adventure on the road, no misspent money? Come on, Mr. Martin, this guy was your buddy."

Benjamin almost mentioned the girlfriend that Edgar alluded to having, but Betty would have wondered why he had kept this secret from her. Benjamin just shook his head until he realized that Heavy was waiting out his pause. He thought of answering "We stopped being friends longer than it appears" but refrained from offering a button they could push to get him to spill out his guts. Instead he fished in his memory for anything that would satisfy them to advance the questioning to a close. He came up with the day "sometime last year, I'm not sure when, Edgar blurted out his desire to dump his family and start over—but what married man doesn't feel that way in moments of depression? That's how I took it."

Crewcut broke in, "Wouldn't a change of life also involve a change of jobs, a different source of income? Did he say?"

"Edgar didn't talk specifics. He might have said 'leave my family, change jobs, start over.' Something like that."

The formerly civil Crewcut then lunged, thrusting his index finger into Benjamin's face. "Look, Mr. Martin, for more than a year before his death your best friend Edgar, an apparently middle-class, upright citizen just like yourself, was also secretly associating with the people on this list, whose business was selling cocaine."

Crewcut's analogy and obvious inference shattered what partition Benjamin fancied he had been creating between himself and Edgar. Sensing danger, he elaborated that "Edgar had only talked generally, about having 'to save up money and be free.'"

Heavy stepped up to the plate: "Didn't that make you curious about what he meant?"

"No."

"You didn't ask what he meant?"

"No, he had stocks he could sell, a retirement account. He didn't go into details. His intention was to tell me that our friendship would be changing and that our wives would be affected. They had become best friends. From that, I just figured that he was leaving his wife, that's all. Hey, cocaine and Edgar? I don't jump to make that connection."

Crewcut picked up the list from the table. "Let's try this again. I'm going to start reciting names. You free-associate and say whatever comes to mind."

This time, primed by fear of being mistakenly planted into Edgar's sorry life, his memory offered up some cloudy rumors he had heard about the first listed name. The other name he recognized was of a fat kid whom the other kids taunted and who later dropped out of school. He didn't recall the others.

"They all lived on your block. You hung out on that street."

"Only up to the eighth grade, and not with those kids . . . Hey, you told me over the phone you had files on these guys, so what do you need from me?"

Heavy interrupted, "You don't remember anybody but others remember you. It was Edgar's mother who suggested that you of all people would know her son best because you were so close, like brothers. I understand you guys were even related, isn't that right?"

Betty's eyes opened wide.

"Who told you that?"

"Edgar's mother was emphasizing how well you two understood each other from the first time you met. She brought up that when your family moved to that block, your mother stopped to ask her about the Bonjour family name. Your mother had come across it only once before, when she read through old papers in Puerto Rico and found the marriage certificate of her paternal grandparents. It seems that her grandmother's maiden name was Bonjour."

"So how does that make Edgar and me related?"

"As your mother said to Edgar's, that is a rare Puerto Rican name, isn't it, and there's only one island family tree with that surname."

"Look, we moved to that block when I was four years old, and since then I never heard my mother say that our families were related."

"Well, that isn't important. The point is that you two kids grew up very close and pretty normal for the environment."

"What does that mean?"

"I mean that you probably got into trouble like other kids on your block—the usual preteen stuff, stealing fruit, shoplifting candy. Isn't that true? When you were sixth graders, you two were picked up for jumping over a subway turnstile. Isn't that a fact?"

Betty flinched.

"Who told you that crock? We never stole a thing."

"Somebody we talked to, who thinks you always believed you were better than everybody around."

"And we didn't jump any turnstile. We got picked up, but it was other kids we didn't even know who jumped as we put in our tokens. Then they started laughing at us and at the token clerk, who just saw us as one gang, and the cop took us all in."

Betty showed no reaction, but from that point on, Benjamin didn't care if the detectives believed his answers, only wishing he could decode the beats of her heart. For even he could understand if she was privately piecing together a damning portrait from the innuendos the detectives were plucking out of his past. If he had concealed Edgar's plan to ruin the life of her best friend Jean, why shouldn't she infer that he might also cover up his best friend's dirty business connections or his own "dark" side? Finally he shot up from his chair and shouted that he had told all he knew and ordered the detectives out of his house.

Heavy retorted, "According to his wife, you and Edgar Bonjour came from the same background, grew up together, stuck together to this day. So anything's possible, Mr. Martin."

Benjamin locked the door behind them, and when he turned around Betty had already gone upstairs. He found her at her desk. She had brought work home from her office and needed to get it done before sleeping. The following morning over breakfast their conversation skirted the issue until he asked for her impressions of what she had heard the night before. His question caught her as she was picking up her empty coffee cup and dish. On her way to the sink, she turned: "Ben, I'm still trying to figure out what I think. I just want to know if . . . Look, I can't get into it now."

. . . He was driving past New Jersey's dreary oil refineries. He wanted to hear Betty speak, say anything, divulge her feelings at least in the tenor of her voice. He complained of the abundance of traffic, of the sun's reflection off so much glass and chrome. Betty just stared through the windshield. Give the thing a rest, he told himself.

. . . The two boys were dressed in St. Cecilia's mandatory white shirt and green school tie and lined up on the school auditorium stage to receive yet another commendation card. Benjamin wondered why Edgar, just behind him, seemed uninterested, fidgeting, distracted, but at that moment the nun was calling out Benjamin to step forward and receive his commendation. Later, Edgar explained that he knew that his mother wouldn't be able to afford to send him to college . . .

Jersey's gloomy oil refineries were behind them now, and the green landscape spread out under the bright blue. Well, it was better he concentrated on driving and not think about Edgar, who was dead in more ways than one, he told himself and almost uttered it, catching himself before he committed the foolishness of setting himself up to be answered with more of Betty's silence.

. . . Two bony teenagers stood in their Catholic high school French class, where the French club met surrounded by travel posters of Paris. Both boys had shunned Spanish, that sharp demarcation between themselves and the Spanish-speaking kids, who clung to their parents' culture, which would only anchor them in their dump neighborhood of dim tenements, a set for a movie entirely of extras—like the doomed public high school kids who hung out across the street on Edgar's building stoop, always dancing to a music primitively portable in their heads. They danced and he didn't: that difference epitomized every other between their kind and him . . .

Betty was still absorbed in New Jersey. He took a deep breath of cool, conditioned air, looking far ahead at the smooth slope of highway that leveled out and tapered into the horizon of clouds, which he stopped seeing . . . remembering . . . his dead father, a lanky building superintendent. Shrunken by his thick accent, he was a little man from his meager island. In this culture he was nothing but an animated prop in the background, insignificant to the center action where the real players performed. That's how Benjamin never wanted to feel, always staring at the backs of those players. His father's dilapidated shoulders, broken-window eyes and burned-out core formed a structure that his spirit refused to inherit . . . In Edgar's coffin he would bury the last memories connecting him to that past. That was his real reason for wanting to be at the burial.

A blue sign announced one mile to the next service area. Benjamin was about to suggest to Betty that they stop when a second sign identified the service area as dedicated to the poet Joyce Kilmer, whose poem "Trees" they had memorized in school. *I think that I shall never see / A poem as lovely as a tree.* Edgar scoffed at the poem and referred to Kilmer as "the faggot poet with the girl's name," echoing his own father's macho manner. And only now did Benjamin realize that, when it came to girls, Edgar had really been a carbon copy of his old man, that horny bastard who would talk about women to impress two pubescent boys. For Edgar really didn't have any standards when it came to getting tail. At one time he even took up with one of the stupid, ever-dancing girls who hung out on his stoop. "She isn't up to our intellectual standards, my man, I know, but she's fine," he said, elongating "faaaain" in that macho-black street drawl that made Benjamin cringe.

He let the Joyce Kilmer Service Area pass because Betty had nodded off, her sleep offering a stretch of relief. At least asleep she wasn't thinking about the disagreeable image he was certain she now harbored of him, forgetting that Edgar was responsible for changing everything in her social life, even the way that she now saw her own husband.

. . . For months Edgar had behaved elusively, always away at sales meetings or other business trips. What few times they did spend together were marred by his having changed in ways that Benjamin couldn't put his finger on. Sensing that something was seriously wrong with the Bonjours, the Martins stayed away until Jean pleaded with Betty, begged them to come over for dinner, to be friends as before because, as Jean confessed to Betty, Edgar was also losing touch with her, and their visit might help Edgar return to the way he used to be.

Instead, that became the last night of the couple's friendship. Betty and Jean were in the kitchen as Benjamin yet again tried to persuade Edgar to purchase a life insurance policy. Benjamin listed the same reasons he gave his clients, but with sincerity. Edgar just stared off until he interrupted Benjamin: "I don't care about insuring them. I want to talk to you about something else. Look, we did all the right things, Ben, but I don't feel enthusiasm for it anymore. My wife and sons have become miniature images across a cold distance, as if on a TV screen."

Sensing a conversation he didn't want to have, Benjamin started to get up, but Edgar shot up first. "I know you won't agree with what I have to say, but of all people you have to listen." Edgar then revisited their days as students at NYU in the sixties. "We wanted nothing to do with the Latin students, but those kids fought so the administration would offer minority scholarships like those that made it possible for two guys named Edgar and Benjamin to go to college."

Benjamin had heard enough, but Edgar was insistent, stood directly over him. "We didn't stand with the Latin students, but where were we? The Vietnam War was on, and America was either for or against that war. But we stayed out of the picture, not patriotic enough to support the war and not wanting to align ourselves with those minority darlings of the Counterculture while we got a free ride in college. Let's face it, we were nowhere, without an identity, two cardboard guys in the background. And that's how I see you now, Ben." Then he stopped, contemplative. The remote spark that had been burning down a ten-year-long fuse finally arrived at its detonation: "You know, I think I gave up on you since the day you chose to shorten Martinez to Martin."

Benjamin sat back stunned as Edgar harangued on how little they had known of the world in which they grew up. Over their dreary neighborhood, Edgar superimposed a fantasy Spanish-speaking community in which most of the fathers were like his and only a few were like Benjamin's always drunk father. Edgar spoke fondly of intelligent, decent, normal people who also lived on their South Bronx block, whom as boys they had talked of forgetting, "because we came from a poor class and confused that with our culture. We only saw ourselves through the distorting eyes of this culture. My father may have been a loser in American eyes, but he came from better stock. I have cousins and uncles who are lawyers and teachers, and one was a prominent political leader. My father would tell me that constantly. But I never listened. It took me years to realize that we weren't just the crap we were made to believe from seeing through this culture's eyes."

Benjamin struggled to rejoin calmly. "Yeah, well, you are lucky because my island family came from cow dung. And I once heard your mother tell mine about the Bonjour men's reputation for womanizing and having kids all over the place. She always talked about your dad as if he was a hard-working saint, but my mother once made a crack that told me that your mother knew better. Did you ever notice why he worked practically every day of the week and you still lived in our neighborhood? Where was the money going, Edgar? My mother once remarked that you have a sister somewhere in this city. Did you know that? Or am I just seeing him through this culture's eyes?"

Edgar didn't react. Nothing Benjamin said mattered.

"So is this your problem, Edgar, your bad Bonjour gene? You want to get divorced so you can fuck around?"

"You just don't get it, Ben."

"You with a surname like Bonjour can't criticize me if you've never experienced the setbacks Martinez caused me. Sure, Martinez got me my entry-level job in the liberal times. Then reality set in with Reagan. Shortening Martinez was the right thing, and I saw the results immediately in my new job. And those ethnically proud Latin students? Well, they no longer exist. Today they're all trying to be where we are. Their causes were a fad, like their hula hoop 'revolution.' Latinos corrupt themselves. Face it, Edgar, there's a sickness built into those you call our people. That's why they live their wrecked lives in those neighborhoods, and for them nothing is going to change. If you're looking back to the South Bronx to find some lost key to another life, you should admit it's damn easy to romanticize now, now that you've lived a suburban life and secured the rewards of having broken free. I'm glad that minority scholarships made life wonderful for us, but we don't owe anybody anything. This crazy safari back to your roots is just a midlife crisis. Why don't you just act like a good Bonjour and get yourself a younger woman and have her blow your confusion out of your system?"

"I already have one."

"So I was right. It was a woman that made you go nuts, that brought out your Bonjour seed."

"Ben, you're missing my point. All we saw was a graffiti-covered wall, I know, but behind it were people good as gold. We made stupid choices because of the ideas they put in our heads. I kept my boys from their grandmother. I kept myself from giving her everything she deserved because I was ashamed of being her son. Look, my father could have been a serial killer. That doesn't change a goddamn thing about our worth. Our problem wasn't our kind. It was this country that made us see only the graffiti. I'm telling you, our problem wasn't us. We didn't have to feel guilty about being us. The sickness is in this country."

"Why don't you just leave it if you feel this way?"

"I will, but after I accomplish my plan."

"What plan?"

"I have to accumulate some cash, get to the other end of a long tunnel. I just wanted you to know that things would be changing, to let Betty know. Jean will probably be needing her friendship more than ever."

Eye to eye, in the soundless, tense air between them, their life-long bond dissolved . . .

Edgar was found in a motel, tied to a chair, beaten beyond recognition and finished off with a bullet to the forehead. The *New York Post* reported the revolting details on the second page, next to a photograph of his gagged and bloodied corpse. Traces of cocaine lined the false bottom of his pharmaceuticals samples case.

Benjamin's profound shame kept him from reading the entire news report: Edgar now meant nothing to him, and even driving to the cemetery was redundant. "Just to bury all those memories and out of loyalty to Jean," he thought, steeped in a bitterness that obstructed his responding to the sight of a tractor trailer that sluggishly reentered the turnpike from the right shoulder.

Swerving the steering wheel left into the center lane, he nearly hit a motorcycle whose rider was hugged from behind by a helmeted woman passenger. The bike dodged then speeded ahead of the braking Volvo, whose abrupt movement awakened Betty. She opened her eyes at the moment that the helmeted woman looked back angrily, giving them the finger. Gothic letters on the back of her denim jacket spelled "Latin Angels M. C."

"What happened?"

"I almost hit them."

Settled into the center lane, he looked in his rearview mirror: behind him roared a motorcycle hoard several rows deep and beyond the edges of the rectangular mirror. Suddenly one pair darted ahead in the fast lane to his left. Another pair did the same to his right. As if choreographed, two more pairs then raced ahead from right and left to converge in front of him. Their car enclosed in a sixty-mile-an-hour cage, Benjamin and Betty were subjected to a barrage of shaking fists, erect middle fingers, hands on groins and roar-muffled obscenities. In the midst of this assault, they heard a crash inside the car: the rear window was shattered. In the side-view mirror Benjamin saw that a cyclist was raising a thick chain to strike again. A second blow punctured the rear glass causing a fist-sized hole. The humid heat quickly displaced the conditioned air.

The chain wielder was a fat Nazi-helmeted rider who chauffeured a woman in a sidecar. From under her helmet, her black hair
flailed in the wind as her fat driver moved up to the Volvo, twirling
the chain as he positioned his cycle beside Benjamin's windshield.
Just inches ahead of a trailer truck whose blasting horn was chasing
off his brother cyclists, the fat rider attempted to whip the chain
against the windshield, but Benjamin braked lightly so the chain
struck the hood. Fortunately, a long penetrating trumpet from the
pursuing truck spooked the fat rider to pass the chain over to his
sidecar passenger and blast off to catch up with his gang.

Benjamin passed to the right lane and slowed down, continuing to drive in a speechless daze until Betty begged him to stop. He
pulled over to the shoulder, stepped out into the suffocating heat
and helped Betty out of the car. She rested her head on his shoulder
and began to cry. She wanted them to forget the burial and go home.

"We're almost there. Jeannie is expecting us. You especially. We'll
stop at the next service area."

By the next service area Betty had regained her composure. So
when he turned into the parking area, she started to suggest that
they drive through and go on but gasped in mid-sentence and
pointed all around the lot. The majority of slots were occupied by
pairs of motorcycles.

A half hour later the Martins were walking a rising path, travers-
ing rows of tombstones. Near the top, behind the last row, with a
wide unused area behind it, Jean stood between her sons Michael and
Vincent, who didn't even look like brothers, one dark, the other fair.
Behind them, a priest consoled a small gray-haired brown woman,
Edgar's mother, who at the sight of Benjamin ran up and embraced
him in tears. Jean introduced Father Nunzio, a short dapper-looking
man who wore a black silk suit and a toupee. The circumstances of
Edgar's death were so appalling that nobody else was expected, so
Jean asked the Father to begin.

Everyone surrounded the coffin that rested on the automated
belts that would lower it into the hole as Nunzio positioned himself
at the head of the casket. He was flipping through his little prayer
book and seemed to find the exact page when a roar turned the
mourners heads to see, in a winding slither now coming up the path,

a long snake of motorcycles. In the mourners' dumbness the leading chrome-bright cycle rolled right up to the grave site. Behind him, cycles parked wherever, crushing flowers, except for the cycle with the sidecar, which only fit on the clear lawn behind Edgar's plot.

In the intense quiet of the engines switched off in unison, the leader's woman threw off her helmet and dismounted to go help her sobbing, long-haired girlfriend out of the sidecar. Her helmet removed, her long black wavy hair wafted in a gust. Shapely in leather pants, she had stunning green eyes set in a smooth, cinnamon-complexioned face. Momentarily forgetting who she was, the gang she belonged to, all the things she symbolized for him, Benjamin was momentarily weakened by the sight of her.

Arm in arm, the surrounding mourners invisible to them, the pair approached Edgar's coffin. As the collective attention focused on the women, Benjamin looked over the leader, who had removed his helmet and looked around, eyes covered with mirror-reflection sunglasses. He was mustached and shorter than he appeared mounted on his huge bike. He also sported a ponytail, which made him look much younger, but he was clearly no kid, looking older than the rest of his gang. Bearing his blood-red helmet in the crook of his arm, he went up to Benjamin.

"We know each other, right?" He smirked.

Benjamin stonewalled, his sunglasses aimed at the women huddled before the coffin. The leader reached out to remove Benjamin's glasses but was stopped by a raised forearm. Benjamin removed his own glasses, willing to confront the leader squarely. But in the sudden flash of sunlight, his effort to stare back defiantly amounted to a pathetic squint. Double miniatures of his own grimacing face were mirrored in the leader's mercury-bright lenses, insect eyes swimming deeply into his own.

"What do you people want here?" Jean shouted, marching toward the coffin. As she passed the leader, he grabbed her wrist. Her sons' reflex reaction was frozen by the entire gang's advance, itself held back by a wave of the leader's hand.

Crying out Edgar's name, the grieving woman threw herself on top of the coffin. Seeing that, Jean pulled her arm free from the leader's grip. Father Nunzio leaned over to touch or speak to the woman but was bear-hugged from behind. Gang members flashed knives or swayed chains to enforce their order to step back, widen the hemisphere of space around the woman. Face down, her hair cascading over the coffin's side as she tenderly kissed its glazed surface, she slid her fingers along the edge of the lid covering the face and seemed about to lift it until the leader gave an order in Spanish, and the fat cyclist plucked her up by the waist. "No, no, please, Joey. Let me stay, please, a little while, a little while." Her hair flailed as the huge cyclist stuffed her, still kicking wildly, in the sidecar. Joey's woman ran to the sidecar and hugged her.

Another order in Spanish freed Father Nunzio. A hand signal disbanded the phalanx of knives and chains. Turning to Benjamin, the leader said, "Edgar talked about you. I remember you. Hey, Tito, you remember this guy?"

The fat guy in the Nazi helmet answered: "Yeah, a snobby kid. Always thought he was *un blanquito*." Tito also wore a ponytail, most of it grey, with a hairline receded back to the crown of his head.

"I think you people should be ashamed of yourselves," Betty blurted out.

"Well, I think you're wrong, lady. He left that woman in mourning, so she has a right to grieve. What do you think, Benny?"

This time, accustomed to the sunlight, Benjamin was able to glower at the smirking Joey, but no words came out.

Joey smirked. "*Adiosito,* Benny."

Benjamin's stare trailed Joey's strut to his cycle. Mounting, Joey erased his face with his helmet's black visor. Both his hands gripped the handlebars as he jumped on the starting pedal, simultaneously igniting the jagged roar of twenty-odd engines. His woman ran to mount behind him. Benjamin expected a sweeping hand gesture, a command to the brigade in keeping with Joey's histrionics, but the skinny leader simply took off and down the path, and the gang roared behind, between tombstones down the slope, racing to recompose the serpent of cycles.

In the sudden peace, Jean fell to her knees, covering her face. Nunzio hurried to comfort her. Betty went over to put her arm around Edgar's mother, who sobbed uncontrollably, repeating in Spanish that she couldn't believe that those people showed up.

But Benjamin felt no sympathy for that woman whose son had cast him into the B-movie life of Joey and his gang. Joey Acevedo was the first name on the detectives' list. That fat rider was Tito González, the other name he remembered. And now before Betty's eyes they had come back from the dead to give credence to the detectives' insinuations.

Jean gained control of herself and approached the casket. She snapped at Nunzio. "Father, can we please finish this?"

Nunzio offered Christian wisdom that begged those gathered to forgive Edgar for his errors . . .

Not expecting to be forgiven, Benjamin watched the coffin descend. That gene in Edgar's blood had done its collateral damage: ironically not Edgar but Benjamin, who most despised their past, was the one who survived to wallow in it. He threw a fistful of dirt into the cavity, then looked up. Betty walked in his direction, toward the man she married or the one hanging out on Edgar's stoop, encircled by the dance of Joey's gang.

The Bonjour Gene

Vincent Bonjour pushed open the heavy metal door and instantly realized that his having climbed five flights to this desolate roof in this neighborhood was both crazy and dangerous, but he needed to confirm with his own eyes that Robert was seeing Magda. Looking around to make sure he was alone up there, he crossed the roof to the waist-high wall that faced the street. Once there, he spun around and panned the black, tar-coated roof again, where in the late afternoon light he saw nothing to fear. He removed his backpack and waited to see if Robert would show up.

The roof provided a really nice view of the distant Triboro Bridge, its lighted twin peaks plotted in white dots against the dusky sky. From this height, too, the slummy-looking block looked cleaner, and as the declining sun of this Indian summer reflected from the highest windows across the street, a golden line of glare ran spectacularly for the length of the block. Vincent took in the facade of the single wall of connected buildings, their vertical and horizontal rows of windows a gallery of picture frames, many with animated portraits of old people, teenagers, and housewives.

He leaned over and took in his wide-angle view of the street. On the sidewalks, children jumped rope or chased a rubber ball or simply each other. From the far end of the street arrived the faintly audible shouting voices of a stickball game in progress. At the nearest corner, men and women that a subway had just returned from work turned and paraded before him to their respective buildings. Seeing them as he felt a cool rooftop breeze, he thought of the lines he had underlined the day before in English class as his professor lectured on Wordsworth's "The Prelude": "Whate'er its mission, the soft breeze can come / To none more grateful than to me; escaped / From the vast city, where I long had pined / A discontented sojourner . . ."

Except he *was* in the city, in the grungy South Bronx, and Wordsworth surely didn't have a crosscurrent of *salsa* and *merengue* swirling around him—although not as loud as the rap music that had just started playing directly below. It came from a suitcase-sized boombox on the stoop of his grandmother's building directly across the street. The boombox was playing next to a guy sitting on the top step of the stoop and talking and gesturing to a one-legged guy on crutches, leaning against the fender of a car straight down on Vincent's side. That one-legged guy had to be Rafy the Vietnam Vet. Contemplating those two, Vincent was reminded where he was and what a stupid thing he had done by even showing up in this neighborhood to surprise Magda and now being on this roof.

Slam! The heavy metal door on the roof of the adjoining building had just shut behind a man and a little boy. The boy's entire body was shielded by a plastic Power Rangers kite. The man took the kite from the boy and carried it toward the roof's front wall. The boy unspooled from a roll of line in his hand. The man, his back to the roof wall, raised the kite with one hand, shouted "Ready," and as the boy ran a few passes back, let it go. The kite wafted briefly before teetering-tottering back down. The man picked it up and ordered the kid to wind the line, move forward, and be ready to run back really fast. Held high by the man a second time, as the boy ran, the kite caught the wind and was blown aloft . . . Like him, as if Magda had just puckered her lips and exhaled a gust that set him sailing up on this roof, with no hope of having her and without a best friend.

Robert had been like his second brother at Fieldston. Last year they entered Columbia together. By identifying with Robert as he habitually did, Vincent tapped into his friend's fair-haired confidence. When Robert moved in on the Latin scene to meet Latin women because he thought they were the sexiest looking, Vincent couldn't agree more. Everything else about Latin students they privately mocked. They felt superior to the Josés, Manuels and Titos with their sleazy mustached look, their ghetto English that always just sounded black, all studying on minority scholarships—which Vincent's mother didn't want him to apply for and wouldn't allow him to accept. Against that slim competition, Robert theorized that those hot ladies were also hot for social mobility and a better class of man, how also Vincent saw himself.

But Vincent and Robert were considerably different from each other. Robert spoke Spanish fluently. His diplomat father had been stationed throughout the Americas, where Robert grew up in Chile and Uruguay. And so his movement between the cultures was not cluttered with Vincent's halting insecurities and second thoughts. If Robert hadn't taken the initiative to join the Spanish Club, Vincent wouldn't have joined because, to begin with, his Spanish was clunky, and socializing was going to be a chore. At Fieldston he had taken French. Now he would have given anything to speak good Spanish, just to be able to defend himself against the Spanish Club snobs who expected that, because he was half-Puerto Rican, he should speak it.

Robert didn't have those problems. The Spanish Club welcomed him. He even possessed the confidence to try to join the more militant Latin Students Association even though he was given the message that he wasn't wanted. The LSA consisted mainly of radical chic gringos and working-class Latin students who used their campus roles to fantasize having the power they were denied in the real world. They didn't care for anybody like him or Robert who came from private schools. Actually, the thought of joining the LSA was the farthest thing from Vincent's mind until he learned that Magda, the president of the Spanish Club, was also a leader of the LSA.

Coming up to this roof was really pointless, he realized too late, and now his sugar was dropping. He picked up his backpack and groped around the books until he found the hard candy. As he sucked on the candy and looked out on the street, he heard the boy with the kite complain that he didn't want to stop. The man was spooling the kite line. It was getting dark, he said, making Vincent suddenly realize it too. The setting sun still dimly lit up the roof, but below the streetlights had turned on, and the lighted apartments were sharply visible through the windows. He could even see into his grandmother's apartment. She was in the kitchen, stirring something in a pot.

Vincent had eaten her food only a few times, never forgetting the roasted pork loin one Christmas. As they grew up, his father stopped taking his sons to visit her, and they never felt compelled to see her on their own. He couldn't recall ever looking directly at her, studying her, as he was doing now. What irony. Magda had told Robert about Rafy the Vietnam Vet, the one-legged drug dealer who hung out on the stoop two doors from her building. Robert passed her address on to Vincent in case he wanted to score some pot. Vincent kept it to himself that his grandmother happened to live on that street, and now the only building that happened to have its front entrance open on that block was across from her building.

Slam! The man and kid were gone. Vincent looked around the quickly darkening roof. Anything could happen up here in total darkness. He had to quit his slumming and get back to his real world, to the West Side and Columbia. He took a last look at his grandmother's window. Behind the sofa, she was having dinner with a younger, heavier woman. What must they be talking about? What was the world of Abuela Martina, that gray-haired dark-skinned woman whose blood ran in him and whom he hardly knew. Of her two grandsons only he was burdened with her brown complexion, closer to his father's. Vincent's brother Michael inherited the blondness of both their Irish grandfather and their Bonjour *abuelo* who, like both his McCartin grandparents, died before Vincent was born. Of his Bonjour grandfather, he had known only a face in a wedding photograph. In its yellowing sepia, his dark *abuela* also looked blond.

Whether the young, golden woman in the photograph or the old dark woman in the window, he found it hard to imagine himself umbilically connected to his *abuela*. What did he receive from her besides her color? He could cite no folklore nor bedtime stories passed on by her. Neither he nor his brother ever called her to chat. Nor she them. Their times together in memory were all tinged with a gray solemnity. His father never forced her on the family. The reason for her disappearance from their lives remained his father's secret. The last time he saw his *abuela* was when his father died. At the funeral parlor and then the burial she was so broken up that she seemed hardly even present. She hugged him and Michael as if in a trance.

If they didn't miss her, maybe it was because they never felt good enough for her. When they were little, she complained that their father had not made them learn Spanish. Admittedly they shunned her, embarrassed that she hardly spoke English, but she struck back as if to say if you won't address me in Spanish then drop dead. One time, because she was sick, his father insisted the boys accompany him to see her. She didn't appear that sick and wasn't very loving or grateful. Their coming down from nice Riverdale to this part of the Bronx was a psychological chore, but she never displayed an ounce of sympathy. Instead she looked at them as she always did, with a kind of shame, exhibiting no sense of being their source of embarrassment in their world, in which her bloodline elicited from others a look that enveloped them in an isolating cellophane.

Afterward he complained about her attitude to his mother, who considered herself "an American, just that," and whose only Irish past to speak of was embodied in a brother in Philadelphia, who visited them every couple of years. Losing patience with Vincent, she lectured him that his identity concerns were a waste of energy, only destined to drag him down. "You're an American like me, that's all." Then what was he supposed to say his father's last name was? "Tell them it's French, that's all, Bonjour is French."

She would say this and then contradict herself by constantly reminding her boys of the history of the Bonjours told to her by their *abuela*. According to her, the Bonjour family line began with three brothers from the south of France, probably French-speaking Catalans. They landed on Puerto Rico who knows when and were apparently very handsome men who married local women and later started other families with mistresses.

His *abuela* claimed that her urgency to pass on that story burgeoned from a fear that the time might come when her husband's Bonjour genes would drive her grandsons to pursue a girl from that little island famous as a gold mine of pretty girls, only to discover that they have committed incest. But after what his father did, Vincent's mother realized too late that the story was really meant as fair warning, that if she insisted on marrying him, Edgar would betray her one day.

Now Vincent's mother repeated the story of the Bonjours in anger, cursing Edgar for hooking up with that young gang girl and cursing his *abuela*'s censoring out that the lineage also apparently carried a madness gene. For Jean McCartin refused to believe that in his right mind Edgar would have squandered a good family and the respectable life he had built for a suicidal adventure. Once, after several glasses of wine, she even made fun of the Bonjour story. What else but madness would explain that those three brothers should leave France to follow the legend of Puerto Rico's being the place to find a beautiful wife, then settle in that stifling tropical heat to screw like bunnies if they weren't out of their minds.

Vincent once tried to impress Magda with his mother's French blood story, leaving out the madness part. But Magda never showed any reaction to anything he said. The one time she ever acknowledged him at all was that very afternoon when she opened her door and just stared at him as if disbelieving that he was actually present. Until that afternoon he had thought the gap between them was cultural. She was the president of the Spanish Club, member of the Latin Students Association's governing board, organizer of protest marches in favor of every radical cause, Latin American Women's Rights, Puerto Rican Independence and the Hispanic Ad-Hoc Committee on Fairness in Admission Practices. But he truly felt that he could sympathize with her causes.

Arresting his attention, she always wore a dress or skirt that revealed her full, proportioned legs. Her long ash-blond hair, halfway down her back, bounced with her constant exuberance. Her every gesture excited him. Her magnetism inspired him to overcome his insecurity among Latin students. Just to be close to her, he labored hard to construct a span across the cultural ocean between them, plowing into the Intermediate Spanish course he had taken just for her (which Robert also took just to boost his average) and practicing for hours in the language lab. He also signed up for every elective on Latin American culture and literature that she took, suffering unable to speak, to let the words come out of his mouth to say how he was feeling.

He wouldn't have minded at all coming to these streets to take her home and now imagined Robert sitting in Magda's living room, holding her hand. Maybe her mother was about to serve fried green plantains and pan-fried steaks with sautéed onions and white rice with red beans, a dish that his mother prepared so deliciously. After dinner the slumming Robert surely will discuss his future career plans, giving an Oscar-quality performance. Vincent's jealousy ignited his heart, which was about to flare up before he took control and realized that he had to purge his soul of Magda and Robert, begin a new chapter, make new friends.

Vincent concentrated on the silver-bright Triboro Bridge against the blackboard of descending night. Just another girl, what the hell, just another girl. He picked up his backpack and turned, only to stand frightened by the roof's moonlit darkness, which he hurriedly crossed. But as he opened the roof door, he heard voices resonating in the stairwell. He waited for the voices to trail off into some apartment, but they only became louder as they climbed to the top floor.

He closed the door slowly, thought of running across the roof and jumping over the low wall that separated adjoining buildings, but the voices were already just behind the door, so he ran behind the eradicating shadows that shrouded the base of a large chimney beside the roof wall. Nothing happened for a long stretch, as one voice behind the door did most of the talking until the door finally opened.

Out onto the roof stepped a guy carrying a silent boombox, the same guy who had been listening to rap music on the stoop across the street, who set the box down and held the metal door open with his back. After a few seconds, through the door came Rafy, who incredibly had climbed five flights on crutches and now hopped out into the triangular light from the stairwell. As Rafy stood in the light, his boombox friend disappeared behind the door, tying it to something to keep it open, and produced a milk crate, which he placed at the edge of the light. The crate was for Rafy, who sat, lay his crutches beside him, and immediately pulled on the velcro strip that held together his rolled-up pants leg.

Boombox kneeled beside the pants leg and spread it flat. Out of pockets sewn along the inside, he removed an inventory of small manila and plasticine envelopes and an assortment of vials. He straightened his torso and took out of his side pants pocket a wad of bills and a small note pad. He counted the bills, wrote in the pad, then returned both into his pocket. Out of his back pocket he took out a folded knife and whipped out its blade. Tilting back the boombox, he wedged open the right lower speaker. The grid popped off. The speaker was smaller than the cavity from which he removed some merchandise and stuffed it into the appropriate flap-covered compartment in Rafy's pants leg.

Vincent's sugar dropped again. He needed to suck on a candy but was afraid to move. In the oncoming daze, it occurred to him that these two guys were culturally connected to him, they being the grim picture he saw when he contemplated his Latin half. Lucky Robert had known a better kind of Latin. That's why he had no problem with getting close to them. But his *abuela* really wasn't Rafy's kind of Latin. And his father wasn't, at least not how he remembered his father, although now he wasn't sure who his father was. Near the end of his life, his father seemed not to care for anybody and looked at his family the way Vincent was observing Rafy and Boombox. Was that distance in his father's eyes the Bonjour madness showing itself, taking him away from his middle-class life to be with that young girl and her drug-dealing gang? What suicidal gene caused his father to gravitate back to this neighborhood and these broken people so he could get killed by them? And now did his father's sick gene have plans for him, the Bonjour disorder that married his mother's hypoglycemia, the inheritance causing his head to spin in a low-blood-sugar vertigo?

Boombox commented to Rafy about a white guy who had come to this block to score some pot. Boombox had made the sale, then gave a sign to Rafy, who, standing across the street, went into the hallway to get the stuff from his pants leg. He came out and, apparently as per their routine, sat against a car to drop the envelope on the curb beside a tire. But this time a patrol car was coming up the street. Boombox whistled. Rafy hobbled into his hallway, and

Boombox vanished into his. The white guy panicked and yelled into Boombox's hallway that he'd come back for it later. Boombox was laughing because that guy, Bob, thought the street was some K-Mart with a layaway plan. "He left his shit on the street, man, he fucking gave it away," as far as Boombox was concerned.

Their restocking done, now they were sharing a joint. Boombox sucked fervently on the roach as he looked down from the roof wall. He was fat with a bushy Afro. He wore a white T-shirt over a pair of baggy, pink knee-length shorts. His high-necked sneakers were loosely tied. He looked up and down the length of the street. Then, bursting out in laughter, he pointed down and looked back to Rafy because that white guy was back, coming up the block. "One unique dumb fuck coming back to K-Mart." They both cackled wildly at that. Boombox described Bob's motions in front of the building across the street. Bob went into the hallway. He came out and looked around. He crossed the street and looked along the curb. "Guess what? He didn't find nothing." They cackled. Now Bob was going back down the block. Boombox also spotted a couple of regular customers coming. He returned to Rafy. "We better go downstairs and do some business." Boombox held the crutches upright for Rafy, who mounted his armpits over the pads. Boombox put away the milk crate, picked up his boombox and untied the door. The metal door resounded like a gunshot, leaving the roof in grey moonlight. After a short while Vincent heard loud and pounding rap beats.

Drenched with sweat, Vincent came out of the fetal position he had assumed in the shadow. He sat against the roof wall and felt through his backpack for a cellophane-covered candy. He sucked and bit into one desperately. He waited for the sugar to kick in, which it instantly did, soothing his entire body, bringing on a mild sedation, in whose comfort the only thing he thought about was the name Bob.

. . . Over her stereo playing a cut by Rubén Blades, one of the few Latin singers he knew, Vincent had to identify himself three times at Magda's door. Her repeating "Who?" to herself cut deeply into his confidence. When she finally opened, at first speechless, instead of inviting him in she demanded to know why he was there.

He asked to be let in. She warned him that she was waiting for Bob. Bob who?

"Your friend."

Vincent had always known Robert as Robert. He hadn't expected this downturn, not in a million years. Robert knew how he felt about Magda. Nevertheless, Vincent kept to his plan. He needed to talk to her—could she lower the volume? As she did, he sat on her sofa, sensing the need to talk fast. She stood with arms crossed, waiting. He explained that he was brought up very different from her, that because of her he had taken Spanish and joined the Latin American Students Association and was willing to—

Magda cut him off. "What are you getting at?"

"Because of your commitment and sense of identity. You're like the star of everything Latin, Magda, you know that."

"Well, so what?"

"I just thought you saw me as some assimilated guy from Riverdale, and I wanted to get close to you. I was ashamed I couldn't speak Spanish fluently."

"And what if you could?"

"Then you would pay some attention to me. I like you a lot, Magda."

Magda rolled her eyes upward and reached for her pocketbook on the sofa. She sat as she took out a pack of cigarettes. Shaking her head, she opened the pack and lit up. She started to speak but paused. When she found the right words, she spoke looking at her lap, as if speaking to herself, the red-tipped cigarette punctuating every word, "I just told you I'm waiting for Bob. Wasn't that enough."

"I didn't know that when I worked up the courage to come here. And right now I don't care."

"I'm going to tell you something, Vinny. I'm going to be frank with you." She took a deep drag, blowing out the smoke hard, her eyes toward the window. Her long hair wore the bright afternoon light coming in through the blinds. Her blue eyes were Bermudan coves in travel posters. She began the next sentence with "I . . ," but paused, then started again, this time looking into his eyes for the first time. "I don't go out with Puerto Rican guys. Okay?"

His words flowed out thickly: "Bob only likes Latin girls because he thinks they all look like sluts. Those are his words, Magda."

"Well, I'm no slut, and he knows it. So I think it's just better if you get out."

. . . Downstairs Rafy and Boombox were back at work. The asphalt looked smoother and peaceful in the yellow street lights. Some kids still played in the dark. A mother leaning out a lighted window hollered out the name "T-o-o-ony." A kid answered her from the sidewalk. Across the street his *abuela* sat in a sofa that faced the window. Beside her sat a younger heavy-set woman. They were watching TV.

Vincent picked up his backpack but stopped to look at the horizon of street lights illuminating a labyrinth that, for him, had no exit. Others had paths that led them to an exit. His grandmother's path led to her island. His mother could walk out to wherever on the planet she wanted. Of course, Robert could too, and now Magda wanted to borrow that freedom. But where did Vincent's path lead? Today he learned from Magda that being this thing "Puerto Rican" meant really being from nowhere, running around this maze, carrying his mother's sugar condition and his father's horny gene—and his *abuela's* darker skin. So what was his dad's path? He couldn't go back to the island like his mother. Did he marry an Irish woman because he didn't have a path of his own? Was his father's only inheritance for Vincent and his brother this maze without end? Was that why he returned to this neighborhood and the people he used to know, to find something he thought he had overlooked when it wasn't there after all?

Vincent pulled open the heavy metal door and stepped into the hall. The soot-darkened, high-gloss painted walls suddenly reminded him of those in his grandmother's building, and in thinking that, the question struck whether Magda had also rejected his being darker than his brother, whether she would have turned away Michael with the same excuse. He took one deep breath and one step down the stairs then stopped: he had just done a crazy Bonjour thing over a woman. He raced down the stairwell to find the path that would get him farthest from this, his grandmother's street, and back to Columbia.

Tying the Knot

Face up on Anthony's bed, Michael Bonjour listened to the mandolin trio tuning up amid the engagement party bustle in the many rooms of the Carmelo house. A sick stomach had given him a good excuse to stay upstairs in his future brother-in-law's bedroom and not have to greet the arriving guests, mainly from Cindy's family. Except for Anthony, who studied law at Stanford and couldn't make the party but sent a gift, the entire Carmelo clan would soon invade the house and vast backyard to toast to Cindy's happiness. From his side, there would only be his mother and his brother Vincent, partly the reason why Michael was feeling sick.

For days he had been dreading the arrival of Vinnie and that predictable fraction-of-a-second when the Carmelos all register his younger brother's darker skin. Michael's anxiety over that, as well as over countless more things spinning in his head at that moment, had kept him from eating anything for breakfast or lunch, so the two vodkas on the rocks downed by noon had been heaved up well before the first guests buzzed at the door. The petite Mama Sylvia Carmelo fed him some chicken broth before sending him up to rest in Anthony's room to recover in time for the party. When he got up from the kitchen table, Cindy's dad took the opportunity to quip that "Michael had turned white as a New England Yankee," and diagnosed the stomach problem as a fear of tying the knot.

Mama Sylvia's broth did pacify his stomach, but after lying down for almost an hour he was still unable to relax, and he could hear the extended Carmelos chiming at the door and filling the house. They had come to publicly celebrate this engagement even though they privately whispered disapprovals that could be felt through the walls.

The engagement's public announcement at the highest decibels in the Providence Sunday paper, with a 3″ x 5″ portrait of Cindy, was kept from him as a surprise. He took the clipping out of his shirt pocket:

> Ms. Cynthia Carmelo, of Providence, is betrothed to Michael Bonjour, of Riverdale, New York City. Ms. Carmelo, a graduate of Providence College, is the daughter of Louis and Sylvia Carmelo. Mr. Bonjour is a graduate of Manhattan College, son of Jean McCartin and the late Edgar Bonjour, from the Riverdale section of the Bronx, New York City. Ms. Carmelo is a graduate student at Teachers College, Columbia University. Mr. Bonjour is an executive trainee with Westminster Bank. Mr. Carmelo is founder and president of Pope Costume Jewels in Warwick. Mrs. Bonjour is a graduate of New York University and is presently office manager of the Manhattan law firm Dunkin, Hayes.

High-heeled steps passed by the bedroom door. Knocking on the door to Cindy's bedroom, her middle-aged cousin Nancy asked when the bride-to-be would make her appearance. The door opened, and Nancy expressed exuberant admiration at how gorgeous her cousin looked. Nancy's daughter Rebecca, the hairdresser, pointed out to her mother the special touches she had given to Cindy's hairdo. Nancy reiterated how simply great Cindy looked.

Nancy's voice lacked the sarcasm she customarily leveled at Michael. For the past three years, at some point when she spoke to him she would inevitably reiterate the first thing she said when they were introduced: that his light brown hair and fair complexion weren't anything at all what she expected when she'd been told that Cindy was seeing "a Puerto Rican guy." From Nancy's reaction, Michael deduced that the only detail about him that made a deep impression with the Carmelos was that he was "a Puerto Rican," when he was really also half Irish.

Nancy was the constant reminder of the odorless yet noxious fumes emitted by the entire Carmelo family, murky signs that he had denied to himself for three years but that as the date of this formal engagement approached increasingly became clear as vodka. There were the afternoon drives with Cindy along the coast, taking in the fishing boats, the dunes, the overcast New England skies, on the way to their dropping something off for her father at the jewelry factory. As those stops were always short, Michael never minded waiting in the car. Only recently did it strike him that Cindy never thought of inviting him up to show off the family business. The full implication of his sitting in the car only flashed into his mind that morning.

He stared at the clipping that announced to all Providence Cindy's engagement to someone she never got up the courage to introduce to her father's employees. This didn't so much pain him as leave him pissed off both at the pretension of these Yankee wanna-bees and his own blind arrogance not to have realized that despite his being an attractive young man, embarked on an M.B.A., an executive trainee, and basically a middle-class person, the Carmelos dropped their chips with the common American herd of goofball mythology, seeing him as a "racial" embarrassment.

This crashing consciousness of the family's pathetic vision of him made the idea of marrying Cindy revolting, a suicide drowning in the wide bay of the Carmelos' hypocrisy, which Lou lorded over him under the guise of Yankee moral superiority. Moral superiority, sure, like intentions to have the wedding officiated by Lou's brother, Cindy's uncle Vittorio. Now there was a great example of a Carmelo contradiction. After dinner last week with the family, this priest, who couldn't control his eyes from grabbing Michael's butt wherever it wandered, also couldn't restrain his impulse to comment on how today's young men wore such tight pants that revealed "their cute behinds." That the Carmelos found him so colorful—"tolerate him; he's my uncle," as Cindy played lawyer—especially grated against Michael, who had to endure Lou's lectures on the immorality that, presumably influenced by "Others," the younger generation was raining down on his beloved country.

Vittorio, at least, was no hypocrite and flaunted his gayness with panache, unlike his brother Lou, for whom any allusion to sexuality, even in jest, was sinfully intolerable as if he had taken a New England vow of chastity. The pinnacle expression of Lou's wacko morality engraved itself in Michael's memory on the night that the big *huomo* invited Michael and Cindy to see the Broadway production of *Cabaret*. Horrified at the choreography that depicted Third Reich decadence, throughout the entire first act Lou mumbled and writhed in shameful disgust until Joel Grey's act-ending dance, peppered with gestures of grabbing women's crotches, became the last straw. As the curtain came down, Lou shot up and ordered that they all abandon their choice center seats in the second orchestra row and walk out. The hypocrisy of this trainee WASP, this Italian American Cotton Mather, whose first lakeside New England home was torched by some pureblood Puritan who didn't want any Saccos or Vanzettis for neighbors, galled the hell out of Michael.

Their phony *acceptance* of him, Michael realized just then, was what unconsciously provoked him to present himself as someone considerably more politically radical than he was in fact. Intuiting that Lou's invectives against Fidel Castro were really a mode of venting his dislike of Latins, including the one in his living room, Michael found himself defending Cuba and justifying Latin American revolutions against Yankee imperialism, a posture that prompted Lou's blurting out feelings previously kept in check by his Florentine better nature.

But Michael's darkest offense was committed inadvertently. He once mentioned to Cindy that if he had the financial opportunity he wouldn't mind settling in Puerto Rico. He meant if they were ever rich and could afford a seaside home, as he didn't know much else about the place and saw it as just a big beautiful beach. But Cindy, still in her rebellious phase against her parents, flaunted that possibility. Well, the thought of "foreigner" grandchildren mortally wounded Lou and set off a chain reaction. His anti-Communism and xenophobia melted in the cauldron of his general prejudices against those "who come here to mooch off America" and his specific dislike of his future son-in-law. After Cindy's ill-advised celebration of possibly living somewhere else, any family conversation that even just grazed against some topic of international news would provoke Lou's erupting in a paean on democracy directed, of course, at Michael.

The June night that the Carmelos met his mother should have served to foreshadow this nauseous moment of truth in Providence. His mother had the clarity to decipher the codes in the Carmelos' words and tone, but he was too rebellious and steeped in denial to admit to himself that his mom was right. The meeting took place in Manhattan. Lou invited Michael and his family for dinner at the Waldorf, where the Carmelos arrived with Cindy, who had just finished her masters in education and moved back home. Having not seen her in almost two weeks (although they talked on the phone daily), Michael expected to feel more attraction than he did, but he didn't give the matter a second thought just then. At the oval table, he sat between Cindy and his mother, facing Lou and Mama Sylvia beside the empty chair that would have been for Vincent, who insisted he had to study, something far more important than being gawked at by jerks less engrossed in his being about to graduate from Columbia and deciding on a law school than his being the darker of the two brothers. Understanding his feelings, their mother didn't pressure him.

During the appetizers there truly appeared to exist some hope for this union, but by the main course the *malocchio* was operating full strength. Mama Sylvia sustained her character of the warm, understanding embodiment of equanimity. She even did a splendid job at showing no reaction that Mrs. Bonjour, although nearly her same age, looked twenty years younger than she did, even though that fact was obvious to any human with a working set of eyes, among whom figured Lou. Michael was proud of his mother's looks, her jet-black hair and green eyes and youthfully kept figure. Also in contrast with the laconic Mama Sylvia, his Irish mother talked a blue streak and kept Lou in stitches with her mildly risqué jokes. If the Carmelos had expected Jean McCartin to be daunted, they were wrong; she did what she pleased, as when she married his father.

Edgar Bonjour's name was never mentioned, and any mention of it would have made Michael want to slide under the table and crawl unseen out of the Waldorf. But his father's ghost haunted every second of the evening. If the Carmelos should mention his name, how was anyone going to explain his father's getting involved in drug dealing and being murdered in a motel? Temporary insanity was how the family publicly interpreted the tragedy. In telling Cindy, grasping at a scenario that made sense, Michael embellished that his father had accumulated debts and simply went nuts in trying to get out of the hole. This spin, Michael figured, provided a financial, logical explanation that cleansed the story of its Latin irrationality, turning his father's downfall into a materialistically rational Anglo-American tragedy, one that would sit well with Cindy's parents. But did the Carmelos really buy his explanation, and were they now about to deal that "other" card?

His mother circumvented invoking her husband's name in her rendering of the decent upbringing that a generalized parental "we" had given both her sons. But at one point that "we" provided a window through which Mama Sylvia could satisfy, in her benign, unthreatening manner, her curiosity to know how a young, intelligent, vibrant woman ever made a choice of husband so mined with social liabilities, although the question was varnished more innocently, "How did you and your husband meet?"

To answer that question, his mother first detoured the Carmelos through her Bronx upbringing and her years on Soundview Avenue where, as the population shifted and her mother remained widowed and too poor to move, in time she befriended Puerto Rican girls. From them she learned how to cook, walk and especially dance.

Of her Latin dancing and playing music in the house, Michael shared his father's embarrassment, but deep inside they were both secretly proud of her. Now her flaunting it as part of her shrewd response to Mama Sylvia made him doubly proud. Her brief autobiography had laid a base of self-confidence for when she got around to describing how she had met Edgar at New York University, in an English class, and that, being attracted to him, she found herself showing off how Latin she could be. Then, letting the Carmelos know that she knew the true nature of Mama Sylvia's ostensibly innocent question, she proceeded to zing them by appending that after she discovered the quality of person he was, Edgar surprised her by letting her know that her acquired Latin mannerisms were superfluous because he wanted her for herself and felt—just like herself, she underscored—that as an American he had outgrown paying any mind to the social stigma other people made of his ethnic background.

"His ancestry was actually French," she surprised them. Lou, curious, said nothing but wrinkled his eyebrows. She told them that a woman from a corporate branch in Chicago once called her, having seen her name in a company newsletter. The Chicago woman was a French Canadian whose parents had emigrated from France, and the name Bonjour had attracted her attention because her parents had always said that only one French family bore that name. To this his mother explained that Bonjour was actually her married name and that her husband's family was from Puerto Rico, but that he had told her in their family it was always said that only one family bore the name Bonjour. Not waiting for a reaction, his mother also made a point of noting the loveliness of Mama Sylvia's earrings, which Lou had gotten for her from a wholesaler from Florence.

As his mother spoke, from the corner of his eye Michael noticed that Mama Sylvia took glances at him. He fancied that maybe Mama Sylvia was trying to extrapolate what percentage of his active ingredients came from this interesting woman, his mother. He thought this because his mother seemed to be making everybody feel good about this engagement, going as far as underscoring how happy and relieved she was that Michael had chosen to marry a girl so charming, generous and intelligent as Cindy—an enthusiasm that took Michael by surprise. His mother had never expressed such favor toward Cindy, who blushed and pressed his hand.

Later, on the drive home, however, his mother revealed that although she did, in fact, like Cindy, her effusive praise of the girl was meant to test how compelled the Carmelos felt to respond in kind toward Michael. That they didn't offer more than smiles and nods told everything she needed to know, which was that if she had any control over the situation, Michael wouldn't go through with this marriage, which did not measure up to the high caliber he deserved. "You're lucky that I didn't leave on their laps the reassuring legend about Bonjour men that your *abuela* Martina so thoughtfully laid on me. For your sake I held back many things I could have said about your father, but what matters now is that you think this out a little better, Michael."

But his seeing her wisdom at that moment was obstructed by a determination to finally resist her admiral's control of him, to carve out his own identity, make this major decision on his own, an independence that came at the cost of reacting normally to so many obvious danger signs. Like Cousin Nancy's incessant innuendos and Uncle Joseph's fish-eye looks. Denying their antagonism, his gut reaction had hibernated until now, the engagement party, when he admitted to himself that although the Carmelos did serve him some honey, it was only vaguely sweet and more often whatever else he drank was acidic. His mother had been right all along, and had he only listened to her he wouldn't be suffering a cosmic bellyache.

Cindy had been walking on the beach of the Dorado Beach Hotel. As a birthday present to Lou, Mama Sylvia had convinced the two feuding Carmelo children—Cindy the atheist hippie liberal and Anthony the neo-fascist Catholic conservative—to convene in truce and take part in a two-week family vacation. While Lou and Mama Sylvia and Anthony played golf, Cindy, who had graduated that month from Boston University, spent bored hours alone, usually swimming or strolling along the shore or reading on a beach chair.

On the sunny afternoon starting the second week, Michael, enjoying his mother's graduation present of a week at the hotel, positioned his beach chair near an empty one. When Cindy returned from the water, with her brown hair flowing, her sunburned skin wet and glistening in a two-piece, he fully appreciated her buxomness and earthy, wide hips. He introduced himself and immediately loved her smile. Her smart and warm personality further contributed to her exciting him thoroughly. At the end of the week, she invited him to have dinner with her family. Everyone behaved genuinely charming, clearly pleased that Cindy had found a vacation companion. In that family context, among such obviously bedrock stable people, Michael felt comfortable, more than comfortable, seduced.

But back in New York he discovered that Cindy's participation in that American Dream family life had been a performance. Her real life was that of a flower child who slummed in one of the few remaining old walk-ups on Manhattan's upscaling Upper East Side. As that person, she couldn't stand being with her parents, especially that bundle of contradictions, her father. "While always harping on being an American," she complained, "he tries to control me totally like every Wop father." On the other hand, the ultra–Yankee Puritan, he also expected her to be WASPily dainty and ladylike and never looking "like a real Italian," meaning made-up or sexy. So whether out of conviction or to get even, she vehemently opposed her daddy's politics, "his imperialist support of our raping Vietnam." He embodied, she would repeat, why this country was becoming a drag for her to live in, why she was willing to live anywhere else if she had the chance.

Michael gradually persuaded her to lower her guard, not be unfair to her parents, who were from another generation and who continued to finance her lifestyle and graduate studies despite having to wait months for a weekend visit. What debt she thought her father owed her Michael didn't care to compute, but he didn't see it as insurmountable. As his defense of her parents' best intentions sank in, Cindy began to cast off her constant dirty jeans and boots and began wearing dresses, using makeup in moderation, and shaving her armpits, changes that gradually brought her closer to the family hearth. In retrospect, the new Cougar parked in front of the house for her birthday signaled a renewed beginning of family bonding, and Lou's move to end their relationship.

But Michael didn't make that connection back then, partly because he had been concentrating on making this relationship a serious one and not taking it to where his Bonjour drives had always led him. The temptation to cheat while Cindy was away was ever present during those days of "sexual revolution," but he resisted them, although the greatest threat came from her parents' home, where Cindy's lonely cousin Rebecca visited often. She and her husband had been separated almost a year. Nobody paid Rebecca much attention in part because she wasn't one to keep up with or discuss the latest news and so stayed on the margins of family conversations. But she was also different because she made it her purpose to look sexy, like a "real Italian." He remembered the cold New England winter afternoons when she visited the Carmelos. As Cindy chatted with her mother somewhere else in that big house, Rebecca would make coffee for herself and offer him a cup, then sit and talk about simple things, movies, funny experiences at the mall. It took fortitude to refuse her pretty attention, but his mind was focused on not doing exactly what a Bonjour man was destined to do and ruin everything.

Maybe it was his distraction with that legacy that kept him from decoding the first message of underlying separation, when Michael fantasized yet again about moving to Puerto Rico: "Will I be happy in a place where I can't speak the language, Mikey?" He was surprised but didn't see at that time the real significance of Cindy's shedding her internationalist pretensions and reclaiming her New England Italo-American roots. He didn't want to see what he was finally seeing now, that when they met she had cast him in her personal psychodrama of rebellion that had performed its final act months ago, that he was now an actor without a role.

Someone tapped lightly on the bedroom door. "Michael, Cindy's ready, so you should be coming down." It was Rebecca. When he didn't answer, she asked if he was all right. Cindy, she explained, wanted him to come down and help her receive the guests. He answered that he would be down in a few minutes, then listened to her high-heeled steps fade away from the door.

He forced himself up from the bed and, on his feet, recalled Lou's answer to his formally asking for Cindy's hand: "I had always expected her to marry a *real* American. You should have figured that out by now, and although I'm sure you'll succeed in your career, I want you to know that if you marry Cindy I'm going to make legal arrangements so that she will keep whatever money belongs to her, and if she isn't happy she can go on her own."

In the bathroom, he rubbed soap over his face, then rinsed it off, pausing to stare at his wet reflection in the mirror. Countless threads of emotions converged and interwove to form a tight, irreversible decision in his eyes. The noose around the neck of this marriage was now tied, and there would be no untying it. He took the newspaper engagement announcement out of his shirt pocket, rolled it into a tiny ball and threw it into a wicker basket on the bathroom floor.

His decision should mend Lou's broken heart and, Michael imagined, return the joy in the saddened soul of every Carmelo. But the actual break should come less dramatically, weeks later when he could feign a confession that he had been behaving like a true Bonjour, maybe with "a real Italian." For now, he would go downstairs, head to the bar, and drink into a politic giddiness.

He put on his suit jacket and was about to open the door when Rebecca knocked again. "Cindy had sent me because she can't get away. Everybody is asking about you. Your mother and brother have just arrived." He opened the door. The dolled-up Rebecca was a woman he had not seen before. Her black hair cascaded in curls. Her dress revealed her legs to above her knees. She wore high heels and sheer hose that decorated the sides of her calves with a black, serpentine, long-stemmed rose of lace.

In taking note of all those details, his eyes communicated more than he had intended, and Rebecca gulped nervously. She cleared her throat before asking jokingly if what everybody was saying was true about his being afraid to tie the knot. His sincere answer yes caught her off guard, and she proceeded as if he had spoken in jest, warning him to stop playing the prima donna, because his mother was asking for him. With that, she abruptly swiveled and started to walk toward the stairs. From the door, he observed her walk, and as she took her first step on the stairs, out of his mouth leaped a request that she wait. She stopped and paused, then finally turned. But as he really didn't know why he had stopped her, he just waved off the request and went back into the bedroom, where he sat on the edge of the bed.

After staring at the floor for a few seconds, head in his hands, he looked up and saw Rebecca leaning against the door frame, arms crossed, her presence like an embrace. He asked her to come in for a minute. Arms still crossed, she lowered her look and tapped one foot. After a few seconds, she sighed deeply, then offered her eyes as she requested that, as a special gift to her, he go downstairs and behave, at least in that house, at least on that day.

What We Should Know about the Climb to Heaven

Ariel Zurita was the second illegal who paid Daisy Bonjour to marry him so he could get his green card and, like the first, was also her boarder. In the five months that he lived in her small apartment, they saw each other only once a week. Every Saturday morning, from her kitchen area separated from the living room space by a dining table, she wished him a good morning as he came out of his room, in a bathrobe, to take a shower. When he returned to his room, she would prepare him breakfast then knock on his door, confident that, unlike his predecessor, he would not walk out in his underwear. A perfect gentleman, he would come out dressed and sit at her dining table, where she would not disturb him as he ate his breakfast and read his newspaper. Except for those weekly brushes, each kept a private life. She didn't know what he did with his days, or why he came in late every night or was gone before noon on Saturday to be back on Monday morning.

She had met him that spring, a year after she was rid of Jorge, a Mexican who had entered her life giving every sign of being a godsend because his money helped to pay off the loan she had taken out to ship her father's body to Puerto Rico. But that Mexican's money cost her dearly. The cologne-sweet Jorge turned out to be involved in mysterious dealings, and she lived in fear of a visit by an armed stranger. And he was a *machista*, who presumed his rent also leased her body. The nights she didn't stay upstairs with Martina, the elderly widow of her uncle Javier, she went to bed with a carving knife wrapped in a towel.

So when Jackie, a Cuban co-worker at the dress factory, approached her sewing machine to make a pitch for a Salvadoran friend offering to pay a U.S. citizen to marry him, Daisy said no. Jackie, Cubanly persistent, personally vouched for this man's decency. He sometimes preached at her Pentecostal church. "Besides, how else would you earn good money so easily. Aren't you saving to retire in your own house in Puerto Rico?"

At work's end the following afternoon, Jackie rushed to catch up with Daisy by the elevators. She gave no sign of knowing what was about to happen. On the sidewalk, standing in spring's late sunlight in front of the factory's door, a man in a brown suit smiled as if he knew them both and had been waiting. Sucked-in cheeks gave his Indian face a determined demeanor. Jackie acted surprised and introduced Ariel Zurita. "You remember, the man I spoke to you about."

Zurita offered his hand. "I'm so glad we are finally being introduced."

Daisy threw ocular flames at Jackie, who apologized for having to hurry home to cook for her hungry husband and took off. Left alone with Zurita, she forced a courteous smile.

"Well, it was nice meeting you, but I have to take a long subway ride home." She started to walk away.

"Can I accompany you to the Bronx?"

Jackie must have told him where she lived. This truly annoyed her. "Oh, do you live up there, too?"

"No, but I don't mind."

"I don't think it's necessary."

"Please, I really do need your help." Urgency irradiated from his eyes.

Surprising herself, she let him accompany her. On the subway he explained that in El Salvador opposing the government endangered one's life as much as actually being a guerrilla. Being related to revolutionaries also put you in danger. His brother, a doctor, was a guerrilla officer. Because their family belonged to a social class that should know better, the government was certain to make an example of them. Zurita suspected that the Death Squad would eventually try to use the family to capture his brother. If they discovered his own connections, they would not hesitate to kill him. But because the Squad had yet to make a move against him or his family, the United States refused to give him a visa as a political exile. An American priest helped him get a tourist visa. Daisy listened, enjoying his polished manner and cultured vocabulary.

Zurita's exiting the train with her brought on butterflies. At the top of the station stairs, she was about to tell him he shouldn't bother to walk the three blocks to her building, but before she got the words out he invited her to dinner at the Cuban-Chinese restaurant behind them. His graciousness caught her off-guard, and she accepted. As they waited for the food, she inquired about his preaching at Jackie's church.

"I don't see it as preaching, really. Jackie exaggerated. Maybe once or twice the minister invited me to speak."

The food came fast. The eating and his curiosity about her personal history—her Caribbean background and her life in this country—lengthened their digression from the topic that had brought them together. Over coffee, Daisy took the initiative. "How long do you know Jackie?"

"Just this last month."

"Do you plan to sell drugs? I won't permit it."

He laughed, "No, no drugs."

"Where do you get the money to travel?"

"From my father. He's a retired dental surgeon who now lives on a substantial inheritance. He comes from 'the oligarchy.'"

"Do you have formal training in something?"

"I used to be a lawyer in my country."

"Why did you stop?"

"I got involved in politics. Then I became a professor."

"How do you plan to earn a living? Do you speak English?"

"I can with difficulty, but I learn fast. I'm thinking of driving a taxi, a night shift for a gypsy cab driver, a member of Jackie's church."

Daisy read his eyes. This Zurita was everything Jackie said he was. He was too good a person to have to negotiate a marriage for pay. "Where are you staying now?"

"With other illegals crowded in a basement on the Lower East Side. Everybody who's staying there is selfish and vindictive. A few hate each other and are capable of avenging an enemy at their own and everybody else's expense. I need to move out. Can we get married soon?"

"How soon?"

"Next week. I'll pick up the license this week. I know a Colombian lawyer who can help me."

"I need a couple of days to think this over." But she knew she would say yes.

He called two evenings later. He agreed to her terms of payment and the monthly rent. A week later, she took Friday afternoon off and met him at City Hall. Jackie witnessed. Zurita moved into Daisy's "Husband Room," filling it with his silence and his books.

That first week he established his pattern of arriving late and leaving on Saturday morning for the rest of the weekend. And every Saturday afternoon when she entered his room to clean she only had to vacuum because the bedclothes were always tucked, the pillows fluffed up, his several shirts and three suits neatly on hangers, his three pairs of shoes abreast on the closet floor. The only other things in his room were books, a collection that occupied every free surface, neatly against one wall on the floor, arrayed on the windowsill and the top of the dresser. Books filled the closet shelves and several boxes under the bed.

How could somebody read so many books? And they all appeared to be about religion. Books with glossy photographs of divine Hindu leaders or statues of Buddha. Books on African tribal gods. Books on Mayan temples. Some were in English, most in Spanish, a few, she guessed, were in French, although even some of the Spanish titles she really didn't understand. *Jewish Mysticism. Christian Spiritualism.* But they all made her curious. After vacuuming, she always dusted the books, extending her time in the peace that Zurita's presence had added to this room. If the book she was dusting was in

Spanish, she tried to read something from it, more often finding it over her head.

Browsing in this way, she discovered *What We Should Know about the Climb to Heaven* by Ariel Zurita. According to the brief preface, he wrote it in Venezuela, on the offshore island of Margarita. She couldn't get over her surprise. Zurita had not mentioned that he was a writer. She wanted very much to read it and took the liberty to borrow it, hoping to have it read before he noticed it was gone. Pressing together the row of books from either end, she filled in the missing tooth of its absence. After storing the vacuum cleaner, she sat on the sofa to read Zurita's book.

His Spanish prose was far more hospitable than the impenetrable words of the other books in his room. The introduction, titled "Why We Need to Imagine Heaven," began simply, "Heaven is what all religions help us find. They are our guides and Faith is the glorious mountain. Heaven is the kingdom we see once we climb to the top. But our guides only help us once we have started climbing. Something else motivates us to begin. We come into the world crying inside with this yearning to experience the wondrous vision from Faith's highest peak. Unless we listen and tend to this soundless crying, we will not begin to look for our mountain of faith." She tried to continue reading but couldn't concentrate, hearing Zurita's voice. She went into her bedroom and placed the book on the night table, at arm's reach, then devoted the afternoon to cleaning the bathroom and kitchen.

That evening, as she did every Saturday, Daisy watched television at Martina's. While they waited for Mrs. Graham, the elderly woman from the second floor who always joined them, Martina inquired why Daisy didn't seem herself.

She confessed that her arrangement with Zurita was making her unhappy.

"I don't understand, if he's such a good man who doesn't give you problems."

"That's what I mean. Treating this kind man in a business-like way, no different than the one before, feels wrong. Imagine treating Javier that way, because he's like Javier in many ways." She said this knowing there was a good Javier, the only one Martina admitted to, but knowing of the Bonjour man who also made Martina suffer quietly over the years. From Martina's reaction to hearing her deceased husband invoked, Daisy saw that Martina fully understood what she was feeling.

"Why don't you try to get close to him, make him your guest, cook for him."

But Daisy knew that those Saturday morning encounters were too fleeting. And painful. Their excitement and disappointment reminded her of those minutes of joy on those weekends that her Bonjour father stayed over. He would come out of the shower in his robe and lift her in his arms for a little while, tickling her until tears came out before the coffee was ready. Then he would walk away and not pay attention to her again. After breakfast he would leave to continue his life with his real family, and months would pass until she would see him again. That was how abandoned Daisy felt when Zurita left her apartment, not to be seen for an entire week.

Later that night, while brushing her now shorter black hair before going to bed, she contemplated her reflection in the mirror. She had not studied herself in a while. At the age of forty-six her vanity had become dormant. She would have wanted to be pretty; right now she wished that her hair were again down to her shoulders. As a young woman, only her Indian hair, which reached to the small of her back, used to catch some eyes. Her father, who inherited the blondness of his great grandfather, or so explained her mother, used to call her his "Indita," his little Indian girl.

She thought back to those few loving scenes with her father, who if being twice unfaithful were not enough, spent more on women whatever financial security she and her mother could have had, so they always lived poor, and after years of hearing her embittered mother damn them as epitomized in the Bonjours, she grew fearful of all men. But despite her fear, she almost married once. Her fiancé was an *americano* soldier stationed at Fort Buchanan. He showed her pictures of his family in Connecticut. He even read her letters from his mother, who said that she was anxious to meet her. But then he got impatient with her Catholic chastity, insisting that they not wait until they were married. "That you be more like an *americana*" was how her mother described what he wanted, because according to her mother an *americana* had no moral standards like island girls. She convinced Daisy to be happy to have gotten rid of him because there are many more men who will be interested. And there were, but not good men, and none interested in marriage to a poor girl who was too much a good girl and not really beautiful.

Daisy pressed the sides of her nightgown against her broad hips, then released the gown, resigned. She got into bed with Zurita's book, and his opening sentences again engulfed her in his voice. She reread the opening on the mountain of faith, but from there found it impossible to concentrate on what the words were saying. Maybe because she wasn't accustomed to reading long writings. Or because she was hypnotized by the voice itself. She decided to open the book to any page and read passages. That night she dreamed of standing on a peak as high as Everest and hearing God speak with Zurita's voice.

In the coming weeks, on the subway to and from work and in bed before sleeping, she read from Zurita's book. When a passage especially moved her, she recited it to herself over and over. In time she learned several by heart. Having Zurita so present gave her a solace that soon metamorphosed into sadness. Her devotion to Zurita began to trouble her. She decided to stop thinking about him. She returned his book to its place. She would see him as a good person and no more. The following three Saturday mornings she prepared breakfast, knocked on his door, wished him a good morning and returned to her room, as before, with no other expectations. Later she vacuumed his room and left it immediately. On the fourth Saturday, she forgot her resolve. After vacuuming, she lingered in the room's order. She dusted the rows of standing books, finding Zurita's. She opened it and read sentences here and there, as if drinking at an oasis.

That Monday, before leaving for work, she thought of leaving him brewed coffee but decided against it. At the factory, however, as her fingers rapidly joined zippers to dresses, she broke her self-imposed censorship. She realized that thinking about Zurita infused in her soul the same sense of order that she experienced in his room. In her private silence in the din of the factory, she ran over the list of questions she knew she had no right to ask. What does he do all day? Where does he stay all weekend? What was he doing in Venezuela? Where is he going? Just before lunch break, Jackie came around and wanted to know how Daisy liked living with Zurita, insinuating amorous fringe benefits. Daisy answered insipidly, without interrupting her sewing. She really didn't know how he was. She hardly ever saw him, for that matter. Jackie, on the other hand, gushed with things to say about him. He had spoken again at her church, and he was magic. "I don't know what that man has, but it is very special, and you should feel very blessed." Blessed. Jackie put her finger on Daisy's feeling.

It had taken Daisy those five months to work up the courage to plan a casual, coincidental breakfast together. That Saturday, she rose early, put on a dress, made herself up, prepared coffee and baked aromatic little bread rolls. She hadn't heard him arrive during the night but assumed he was in his room. Late into the morning, she had not heard a rustle. She tapped on his door. Daring to open it, she discovered that he wasn't there and that the room had an air of not having been slept in. She never imagined such a painful disappointment. She changed into pants and trained her mind on her chores: sorting out dirty clothes, purchasing a lottery ticket on the way to the coin laundry, doing the wash.

She pulled her shopping cart with two bulging pillowcases through the Saturday laundry crowd of mostly women and children. No machine was free, a sloshing in every porthole. She waited on the wall-long bench. The woman on her right shouted at a pair of children chasing each other. The woman at her left complained to a friend about her exploitative landlord. Daisy removed Zurita's book from one of the pillowcases and opened it at random. Her eyes, initially at sea, swam to the boldly printed section heading. "Angels, With and Without Wings." Angels, according to Zurita, captain the hands of good works on Earth. "We don't have to wait for our wings to perform our role, if we decide to join God's highest officers." Surprised by her improving ability to retain his ideas, she read on, unable to differentiate who, according to Zurita, was an angel and who merely a good person in life. She was interrupted by the loud mother's reprimanding her two kids for playing tag around and behind people trying to do their laundry.

The washer directly in front suddenly stopped. The woman who complained about her landlord piled her clothes into a plastic basket, then threw the machine window door shut. In the circular window, Daisy's reflection was obese as a Buddha. The business of throwing the clothes into the tumbler evicted the Buddha from her mind. Unable to read Zurita amidst the laundry's distractions, she picked up a copy of that day's *El Diario* that someone had left on the bench. A report on the civil war in El Salvador touched her as if on a personal tragedy befalling Zurita.

Back in her apartment, as she folded her clothes, a bubble burst in her consciousness, revealing the one thing she had not considered: Zurita's woman. It would only be natural that he had one. Even though *she* obviously didn't arouse any curiosity in him, he didn't look like a man who liked men. Her clothes put away, she straightened up in the dresser mirror. She was heavy, but not the Buddha in the washer window. She removed the pins holding back her hair and brushed, extracting some luster. A dab of moisturizer softened her brown skin. A touch of rouge highlighted her cheeks. She was forming a red circle on her arced lips when keys jingled at the apartment door. She went out to the living room. When the door opened, her hand jumped to her heart. "My God, you frightened me." Zurita looked wrong, rigid as a robot. "Ay, did something happen?"

"My brother was killed last week. Government soldiers. My family is in hiding. I don't know where."

"Oh, Blessed Jesus," she said, making the sign of the cross. She wrapped his limp arm around her shoulder, crutching his few steps to the sofa.

"The soldiers went after my brother. They accused my parents of protecting him." His eyes looked ancient. He had probably not slept for days. Daisy went to her kitchen cabinet and returned with a bottle of sherry and a drinking glass. Beside him, she poured an inch of sherry. Zurita thanked her but just held the glass with both hands. His eyelids started to droop. She put her palm under the glass and lightly pushed up, "Drink it." He looked at the glass as if it had suddenly materialized in his hands. As he drank, she stroked wide circles over his back. After he finished the sherry, she put the glass on the floor, and gently pulled him toward her. His head was almost on her shoulder when, losing her nerve, she moved out of the way and positioned it on a cushion against the sofa arm. She stretched out his legs and removed his shoes, then went to her bedroom and called Martina. "He's lying on the sofa like a corpse, the poor thing." After hanging up, Daisy felt lost. Zurita's book was on the bed. She opened to a page near the end and read the first complete sentence. "The commission of angel is for eternity. Each of us, with or without wings, must covet its prestige by carrying out our mission to do good every second of life and in the afterlife, whether as a Hindu, Jew, Mayan, Yoruba, Buddhist, Moslem or a Christian. Every act in the universe, however miserable it may seem in our time, redeems itself in the history of the cosmos; every molecular change is sacred." A well of sympathy for his grief began to overpower her. The telephone rang.

She rushed before the ringing awakened Zurita, then covered the mouthpiece, pausing a second to compose herself. Someone sniffled on the other end. "Hello," a woman asked in Spanish, "Hello, can I speak with Señor Ariel Zurita."

"Well, Señor Zurita is sleeping right now. Would you like to leave him a message?" "No, well, yes. Please tell him that it is urgent he call Marisol Contreras."

The speaker sounded like a decent woman. "If you will excuse me, Señora, but does this have to do with his brother's death?"

"No, well, indirectly. It's complicated. It's extremely important that I reach him soon." A faint voice whispered in her mind and she heard a buzzing, like at a door, only in her heart. "He's sleeping right now. Why don't you come here?"

"Oh, Señora. . . . I don't think it would be correct."

"Don't worry. It's all right. Come over now."

Marisol Contreras lived in Manhattan. It would take her almost an hour. She knew the address.

The invitation from her own lips now struck Daisy as perverse. She did feel sorry for this weeping Contreras woman, but she also wanted to meet her and compare. Intuiting a strong blow, she took a shower, put on the dress she had worn that morning and touched up her face. She was steaming milk for coffee when there was a knock at the door.

Daisy looked through the peep hole and saw a pretty, young pale face. Daisy patted her hair with her hand and opened the door. Marisol Contreras greeted her, holding out her hand. Her petite, proportioned figure was discreetly displayed by her dark blue dress. A matching sweater hung over her arm. Daisy put a finger to her lips and pointed to the sofa. Marisol looked and nodded.

Daisy seated her at the dining table, with her back to Zurita. As Daisy served her coffee, Marisol kept looking back at the sleeping Zurita. The necessary "How dark?" and "How many sugars?" broke the ice and fixed Marisol's attention on Daisy. They spoke in a whisper.

"I don't know if Ariel told you about me. He said he was going to."

"No, but I imagined you existed."

"We met at church. I had just come from Colombia . . ."

"Look, I don't really have a right to know anything. He's a good man, and we have a business arrangement, that's all. You don't have to tell me anything. If you want to wake him, I can let you talk in private."

"Ariel says you are one of those people he calls angels. He tried to stay out of your way as much as possible because he was ashamed he had to impose himself on you."

Daisy didn't know what to say. That Zurita should consider her an angel came as a shock.

"But what I have to tell him may affect you. So you should know too." She paused.

It was hard for her to begin. Daisy, nervous, excused herself, got up and opened the refrigerator. She removed a bakery box and lumped a handful of cookies on a small dish. Holding a cookie between her teeth, she offered the cookies to Marisol, who shook her head.

"I am not divorced yet. My husband refuses to give me a divorce. He is waiting for me to go back to him. He says that if it's necessary he has friends who can provide evidence that I am involved in selling cocaine. Either I go back to him or he will report me. I am supposed to be living alone while I decide. I met Zurita at my church. My husband found out about him and insists it's a long-time affair, that I really left him for Zurita. My husband paid a detective to investigate Zurita. He knows about Zurita's political problems and about your arrangement. If Zurita tries to register as a political exile, he says he'll pull strings so it won't work. He wants to get Zurita deported and is willing to do anything against you and him or anybody. I can't bear to think I can cause so much harm to this man or to someone like you. I was going to run away, tell my ex-husband I had broken with Zurita, then disappear to Florida. I was preparing my mind to do it. I planned to avoid Zurita, but when I didn't hear from him in three days, I started to worry. Nobody at church knows about him and me, so I wasn't informed right away about what happened in El Salvador. Today Jackie told me what happened to his family and that nobody knew where he was."

She was about to cry. Daisy reached over and pressed the back of her folded hands. "Your husband, what is he?"

"Arcadio's a citizen. He's Cuban. He swears the detective can prove Zurita's a Communist, so you can imagine how he feels about getting him deported. Zurita devotes his time to helping his priest friends get persecuted people out of his country. The priests feed him. They give him a little money. He could not kill like his brother, but he has the same commitment. He didn't want you to be afraid, or get hurt because of his work. He was talking of moving from this apartment to protect you from Arcadio."

"And you? What's your status?"

"I have the green card."

Daisy didn't know what to say or do. "Why don't you wake him up. I'll go to my room." As she rose from the chair, Daisy saw Zurita already sitting up. He was rubbing his face as if realigning disjoined parts.

"Daisy, you don't have to leave the room."

Marisol's rushing to sit beside him pierced Daisy with jealousy.

"There's only one answer." His head shook off sleep. "We have to leave together." Marisol's hand was stroking wide circles over his back.

"No." Marisol transformed from a tender nurse to a formidable opponent. "You have invested too much. I don't want these gringos to kick you out." Turning her back to him, arms folded, she fumed determination.

Daisy remembered a passage she had memorized but hadn't fully understood until now: "Angels measure their acts cosmically. If an Angel cups a hand, it may not fill with water for months, decades, or centuries and might take eons to comfort the waiting, burning lips for which that hand was raised."

"You don't understand, my love. Just because you tell him we have separated and then disappear, Arcadio won't believe you. His detective has probably told him every detail of our life together. You'll leave, and after I get my green card, I'll follow you. That will be the logical theory. The only way he can short-circuit that is to get me deported now and that would mean Daisy will also suffer. She can be accused of conspiracy. I can't allow that, and neither can you."

That danger had never crossed Daisy's mind. But even though Zurita described it so clearly, she still wanted to defend him no matter what. Her words came out like breath. "Zurita, please don't worry about me."

"Daisy, my decision is the only right one. With Marisol I know I will survive, but without her I would simply lose my sense of place. I'm not afraid of starting over. Time is endless. I'm just afraid of losing her and not recovering her in this lifetime."

Listening to him, Daisy heard the voice in his book. Zurita went into his room. Daisy listened to the banging of empty suitcases, the locks snapping open. Marisol was now standing, her arms still folded, her stare aimed at the floor. Daisy came up to her and gently squeezed her arms. "If he stays I'll take care of him for you. I don't think you would lose him if he waits until he gets his green card. It's just a question of three or four months. But he wouldn't be happy without you. And maybe he can work things out later on. He has friends who help him. Look, deep down he doesn't care if he lives in this country or any country. He carries the universe inside, you know that. He always has that green card."

Marisol nodded, letting her arms fall. "I should be helping him."

"Oh, tell Zurita that I have his book."

Marisol spun around, rejoicing. "Oh, thank God. He thought he had lost it. It's the only copy he brought with him. And now who knows what happened to the others?"

Marisol helped Zurita, and Daisy steamed more milk. The movements in her "Husband Room" made her think of the days ahead: the couple's deciding where to hide, their emptying out Marisol's apartment, their moving out the boxes of his books. Every foreseen stage excavated an old inner cavity she would have to refill with something else, as she had managed to do all her life. "Who can say," she heard Zurita's voice, "the purpose of a lonely life, a quiet solitude that for years must witness the joys of companionship bestowed on others. A long solitude can be the protracted prologue to a redemption in some glorious future." The words began the process of replenishing his presence. That's when she remembered. Zurita had agreed to pay in full, whether or not he obtained his green card. But she could not accept his money. Instead she'll request, so he'll always know where to find it, to remain the keeper of his book.

Unforgettable Tangos, Indelible Pagodas

"Are you okay?" Martina vaguely heard, but not loud enough to interrupt her rote knitting or call her soul back from where she had taken it, staring off into the summer night through the open window behind the TV set. Transported to the balmy night breezes of her island town, she was young again and waiting for Javier to arrive with his guitar and sing a repertoire of Carlos Gardel's tangos. One of those songs, "The Day You Love Me," *their* song, was the title song of the movie classic that she and Daisy, Javier's niece, were waiting to see after the late news.

"Martina? Martina?" She heard the voice louder now. But why was Daisy shaking her? Why was she asking if anything was wrong? Martina answered, "What?"

"I have been talking to you, and you were not here. Gone completely."

"I'm here. I had been working on a difficult part of my knitting and got distracted."

Daisy reminded her that the Lotto drawing was coming up after the commercial and that they had just announced the night's prize as seven million dollars. Daisy picked up the empty dish on her lap and went into the kitchen, her wide behind looking even bigger in jeans. Mrs. Graham had already nodded off on the sofa, as she normally did at that hour, with her bifocals slipped down to the very tip of her nose.

Daisy returned with the dish piled with more green grapes and yellow cubes of cheddar. She tapped the back of Mrs. Graham's hand, a miniature map crisscrossed with blue and red roads. "Mrs. Graham, the Lotto."

"*Apúntale los números.* Write down the numbers for her." When Mrs. Graham fell asleep, Daisy and Martina unthinkingly switched to Spanish. Daisy put the dish on the floor, went back to the kitchen and returned with a ballpoint and small notepad. She made the sign of the cross before the brunette ministering the lottery. "Today's Lotto numbers are . . ." Up popped the first ping-pong ball. Daisy jotted down the six numbers, then checked her ticket. "Not one. Where's yours, Martina?"

Martina's puckered lips pointed to the top of the set. "But first change the station, Daisy, for the Gardel movie." At arm's length she examined the nearly completed breast piece of the sweater she was knitting.

Daisy stared, shaking her head. "It's uncomfortable to watch you knit a wool sweater in this heat."

Martina explained that she wanted to have the sweater for the fall. But there was another reason. Two weeks before, a man crept up from behind as she entered the building, choked her and grabbed her purse. She didn't see his face or height or color. In her distress, she dialed her son Edgar's number, deliriously expecting him to pick up the phone. But Edgar had been dead for four months. Her daughter-in-law Jean answered. She did her best to console but reminded Martina that her son was no longer alive. Jean offered to visit but, having already faced the painful reality, Martina was getting a grip on herself and didn't think it necessary.

Left to her solitude, Martina reflected on her sorrow. First Javier, and now Edgar. Martina missed them so that she even dared to think of looking up Javier's illegitimate daughter, whose name she vaguely recalled was Rosa Isabel or Isabel Rosa, who had to be a young woman by then. But it was only a fleeting thought. "How could I think of calling her. How could anyone, especially that child, forgive me?" So enraged had she been that Javier would betray her, would behave as they had warned her of Bonjour men, that she didn't think of the children. After having Edgar, her body could not produce another, and he grew up wishing he had a brother or sister when all that time he did have a sister in Brooklyn whom he never knew because of his mother's jealous anger. The mugging so soon after Edgar's death, she came to believe, was part of the great penance she was paying for her sinful behavior toward that innocent girl. Her world had turned into a single cold season, and so she started knitting the sweater in summer.

"Well, you hit one number, 18."

"You better wake up Mrs. Graham because she's not going to watch Gardel in Spanish, and I don't want you or me to have to walk her downstairs so late."

"That reminds me. Martina, can I stay with you tonight? My new 'husband' has been coming home drunk every night this week."

"Of course, stay here. When will he get his papers?"

"Another four months, maybe less. I swear, I'll never do this again. I don't care how much I'm offered."

Martina nodded, sympathizing.

"It's just that I need the money. I am afraid of getting old and not having anything, like . . ."

"You better wake her."

Daisy gently shook Mrs. Graham's thin arm. Her plucked bird's body trembled. Her eyes half-opened. "Oh, I fell asleep."

"Yes, we're going to see a movie in Spanish."

"Oh, did I miss the lottery?"

"I wrote the numbers down for you."

Mrs. Graham inserted her thumb and index finger into her bra near her arm and extracted a lottery ticket. She tilted her head back to read it through the lower bifocals. "No, I don't believe I have anything."

"You know, Martina, Frankie the *bodega* owner says that he sold a winning ticket last week, and the winner hasn't claimed the prize. That person from around here will get a million and a half dollars. Mrs. Graham, what would you do if you won?"

"My God, I don't know. I never thought of the money for myself. I play for my daughter and two grandchildren." Mrs. Graham's daughter came to see her twice a month, if that much.

Her loud voice, always scolding her mother, was audible from Martina's kitchen.

The Gardel movie began. While the credits were still running, Daisy offered from the dish, and Mrs. Graham took a grape and a cube of cheese.

"Is that him? Oh, he was handsome. I'm sorry I can't understand what they're saying." Martina could tell that Daisy was getting impatient. Gardel might sing at any moment, and Mrs. Graham wouldn't know to stop talking. Also, around the time that Mrs. Graham went home Daisy always tired of speaking English. Mrs. Graham owned a television set and came upstairs only for the company. The Spanish movie isolated her. "I should go home before I fall asleep again."

Martina piled the knitting beside the lamp on the side table and took a deep breath before pushing herself up against the arms of the sofa chair. The pain in her back kept the memory of the mugging fresh.

"Martina, you don't have to get up. I can see Mrs. Graham down the stairs."

"I have to get up anyway. I've been sitting too long. You stand at the door and watch out for me." Aided by Daisy, Martina got to her feet then chaperoned her slow, delicate guest out the door and to the top of the stairs. Mrs. Graham descended the stairwell like a child, making certain both feet were on one step before venturing on to the lower one. At seventy-eight, she was twelve years older than Martina, who imagined herself descending in that skeletal body. She waited to hear "Okay, good night" and the lock click before returning to Daisy, who kept a poor watch at the door, her head turned to the set, trying not to miss a second of the movie. Back in her living room before the TV set, Martina watched and knitted as Daisy watched and ate. Neither made a sound until the first commercial.

"Martina, you know we always talk about how nice it would be to win the lottery, but what would you do if you really won. What would be the first thing you would do?"

"I don't know. When Edgar went to college I dreamed that one day he could help me get a house on the island, but that died when he got married and distanced himself from me. Now that he's gone I don't know what I want."

Daisy's obsession with winning money frightened Martina because her own father was a gambler. Her family lived poorer than they had to because of his habit. An odd-job laborer, he spent every cent trying to win at dice, cards, the gamecock arena, the horse races and the island's lottery. One day he won a few thousand dollars, good dollars of that time, and tried to make up to the family with clothes and other necessities his gambling had denied them, but eventually the bulk of the money went back to the prankster god who gave it. Martina spent her life trying to forget that unhappy time and always shunned any games played for money. Only her desire to share with Daisy the brief excitement of the Saturday night drawings softened her into seeing the weekly dollar as a harmless investment.

Now for Martina the mugging was the speaking voice of money's dark side. The following week she purchased the weekly lottery ticket but secretly hoped never to win. Her vulnerability became her foremost thought. What would happen if anyone knew she had won money? The neighborhood would flare up with the news. Strangers would knock on her door to beg or threaten her. She would be imprisoned in her house. She would have to move. Where and alone? Back to the island, to generations of relatives she didn't feel close to anymore? Here she had Daisy, who had become like a daughter, and in the web of Bonjour meanderings, who was the daughter of the woman with whom Javier's brother Nelson had created a second family on the island. She had inherited those hallmark, melancholy dark Bonjour eyes, also Javier's and Edgar's.

Martina shuddered at the thought of losing Daisy now but cringed as much at the idea of winning money that would attract false affection from her daughter-in-law and indifferent grandsons and especially long-lost island relations, who long ago stopped caring about her and her son. And no amount of money would resurrect her joy, buried with Edgar. The police said he had been trafficking in cocaine, that he was found dead in a motel, but Martina refused to believe that account. No evidence was powerful enough to alter her image of Edgar as a good boy who, if anything, gave every indication of having grown up saved from her father's legacy of a lust for money. Instead, she could believe that as a Bonjour he would throw his life away for that beautiful gang girl who came to grieve at the burial.

"Martina, I know what *I* would do if I had money . . ."

Martina read Daisy's pause: stop boarding illegals who paid to marry her so they can earn their "green card." The first "husband" turned out to be a lowlife who sexually terrorized her. That money paid off the bank loan she took out to fly her father's body to the island. The second one was an educated man, with whom Daisy fell in love and from whom she refused to take any money, although she eventually received the full amount. She used that money to purchase a small plot in Puerto Rico, where she hoped to build a house. Now she had a third "husband," an alcoholic, convincing herself that the money for that house was really why she agreed to another unpleasant marriage. But Martina knew better.

Number three resulted from Daisy's attachment to that special number two, Ariel Zurita, a kind, religious man and a writer. During the months he lived with Daisy upstairs, she visited less often, but Martina was happy for her, glad that someone had started a special fire in her. Unfortunately Zurita was unaware of Daisy's affection and anyway loved another woman, the one with whom he disappeared to hide from the immigration agents. Months later she received a friendly note, then a Christmas card, and eventually a money order. But that was the last she heard from him. Only recently had Daisy confided to Martina that his beautiful soul still accompanied her, residing in the book he had written, which she kept by her bed. It was plain that after Zurita she didn't want to live alone. Martina got the idea to invite her to move in, but then Edgar died, and distraught, she herself turned inward. For weeks she didn't want visits from anyone, even Daisy. It was during that difficult time that Daisy agreed to marry that man who always smells of rum.

". . . travel, first. I always wanted to see Denmark and Sweden. I remember the stories we read in school. Cold countries with hard pale Nordic people. And to the Orient. When I was little, a Venezuelan-Chinese family lived in my neighborhood, and the grandmother talked to me of China. Temples, rickshaws, pandas— and pagodas. She showed me pictures of the pagodas. They are indelible in my memory, Martina. I'll never forget how beautiful they seemed to me. And, of course, see the land of Gardel, the gauchos, dance to unforgettable tangos. And buy a nice camera and take many pictures. Then go back to the island and buy a house in the south, near Ponce, facing the Caribbean. And a car, naturally. Ay, this is painful. Oh! Look!" Her wish list had spilled over onto Gardel's return.

When Martina was a young woman, Gardel was the dreamboat of the Latin continents, as mythic to her generation as Frank Sinatra and Elvis Presley in English. On the humid Caribbean nights, his magnificent tangos inspired the young Martina to take fantasy excursions to Buenos Aires. Under a dark blue sky with wet stars, as the louder *coquí* tree frogs upstaged the crickets, Edgar's father played the guitar and serenaded her with a repertoire that always included *"Volver." To return, twenty years later, with a wrinkled face, to an old love, . . .* Listening to Gardel, she heard the courting Javier and forgot the pain he put her through years later. Maybe because it was her fault, because she couldn't give him another child, he took up with one of the cleaning women in the office building where he did maintenance work and had that little girl by her. Martina looked back at her jealousy and anger and felt wrong that she deprived that child of a father by forbidding Javier to see her and have anything to do with that woman again. She never wanted to hear of the money he sent them or that they ever existed: those were her terms when he begged her forgiveness, and that was how they lived, she denying everything else to have his devotion only to herself for the next five years until a cancer killed him.

But all that took place so long ago. Now, on the summer breeze blowing in from the open window behind the television set, on a carpet of nostalgia, her soul floated out above the street to the years before his adultery. From that height in memory, she saw herself accompanied by the young Javier, allowing herself the fantasy of embarking on Daisy's dream tour: Denmark and Sweden, China, Buenos Aires, a trip of thousands of miles with the peace of mind that their house waited for them by the sea.

"It looks like it will fit, but . . ."

Before sailing to Argentina and China, Martina had tried on the nearly finished breast piece and, enraptured by the tango, had left it over her bosom.

"The color. Why did you make it so bright, red-orange? Like the lottery tickets."

"Oh it's not the same color at all."

"Ay, Martina, look!" An airline commercial they hadn't seen before showed scenes of Puerto Rico, of the city of Ponce, where Daisy grew up. Martina's fingers stroked the knitting, feeling for the stiff spot over which she intended to sew on a pocket.

The movie's next segment was brief, ending with Gardel kissing a conniving woman, a long kiss. Martina stepped into the body of that actress, returning his kiss on her porch facing the Caribbean.

"Look, you have goose pimples. What were you thinking?"

Martina examined her arms. "I don't know. I was watching the movie. Then I started to wonder if you would really do all the things you said you would do if you won the lottery. Would you travel to all those places? And would you leave this country after so long?"

"Of course. What do I have here? Just me, now that my sister returned to the island with her kids."

"But you aren't an old woman yet, you can . . ."

"What? Get a man? I'm not interested in hunting down somebody, and I don't want to take care of any man, especially an old man. But I would like to travel and have my own house."

Gardel eventually saw the evil of the woman who had stolen his heart. He sang the theme tango to the right one. Now Javier was playing Gardel, singing "The day you love me . . ." Martina's soul flew across the street to the jutting corner of a roof, suddenly the prow of a cruise ship in the night. To "The Day You Love Me," she and Javier danced on the high seas under an ocean of stars until a cooking oil commercial jarringly ended the spell.

Martina's eyes lingered on the TV screen, not seeing Daisy leave for the kitchen to return the empty dish nor consciously looking at the soda commercial showing a tall drinking glass filled up with clear bubbling soda, although its effervescence rose up Martina's spine. The notion fizzed refreshingly: to trust Daisy with her secret.

Martina wormed her finger into the knitting, then stopped. Can this elation too soon after Edgar's death bring on God's punishment, maybe another mugging? While slowly extracting her finger, she recalled Mrs. Graham's bird-like body downstairs, always alone, caged in her apartment, the way *americanos* abandon their old people. That's how her grandsons will leave her because this country had taken possession of them. Then she thought about Javier's daughter, the sister that Edgar never knew existed, whom her jealousy had deprived of a father and who really deserved more in life. Maybe now good can come from so much hurt.

Her finger penetrated the knitting again, this time writhing to cover itself with the thin cardboard, feeling its reality as she reflected until her conviction came in a rush, and she was certain of doing the right thing. Her decision released the excitement she had been containing since the previous week, when she lied to Daisy that only one number matched, then crumpled the Lotto ticket but saved it, having a year to decide to claim its value.

A symphonic crescendo played behind Gardel's return to the good woman. Daisy sighed profoundly, already on her feet, about to steam milk for hot cocoa. Martina sighed, too. Together, emitting a light just like the one in Daisy's eyes, they will savor the cocoa and, for the rest of their lives, enjoy Gardel, who will sing in their house on the Caribbean after joining them in Buenos Aires, where he will wait for them to cruise down the Pacific on their return from the ice palaces of Scandinavia, from the indelible pagodas of China.

Cappuccino

She always arrived at the midtown food court a half hour before he did, to secure a table as well as to have a little time to herself, gather her thoughts, enjoy a few pages of a novel. But on this afternoon the court was inordinately busy, and she had to use up her cherished, private half hour to find and hold a table for just the two of them. Luckily, while paying at the coffee counter, she spotted a frail woman getting up to help a slow-motion old man with his coat. Careful not to spill the brimming steamed milk from the cardboard cup, she reached the newly unoccupied table and claimed it with her briefcase and purse. This much accomplished, she removed her coat, sat and made herself comfortable.

The first sips of cappuccino were welcomed by her throat and then her entire body, a stress-tightened fist that slowly loosened its grip. Soon feeling relaxed, she reached into her briefcase for her paperback copy of Jorge Amado's *Doña Flora and Her Two Husbands,* and that was when her balloon of tranquility exploded, punctured by the sight of, wedged in the paperback, the lengthwise-folded manuscript of her husband's latest short story.

Manuel Bonjour, a reporter for the Spanish-language daily *El Diario,* had forfeited her respect after squandering too many nights writing stories. When they married, her old Aunt Grace, who knew his family back in the dinosaur days of Puerto Rico, warned her about that family and their men's reputation as adulterers. But he seemed completely different, never staying out late, coming home early every chance he could—but not to be with her. She never expected this kind of betrayal and now bristled when she thought of the mornings when a manuscript of a fresh story written at her sexual expense waited for her on the dining table. A yellow stick-on note always apologized for his going to bed after she had fallen asleep.

In their first year, when she was willing to go to any lengths to make this second marriage succeed, she read his every effort, lacking the courage to confess that they were difficult to follow. She thought she really did love him and recalled that she never felt closer than when he was assigned to report on the death of some distant relation—actually nobody he even knew—whose last name was also Bonjour. The guy was found beaten to shreds in a motel over drugs, and Manuel didn't want to report it, but his editor liked the tabloid irony of his byline flashing the same surname and, of course, insisted on printing the horrible picture of the blood-covered victim. Manuel was just starting out and felt that he couldn't refuse. He lied to his editor and the readers, underscoring that he wasn't related to the subject. But at home he poured out the shame that was killing him because, of course, as he had told her on the day they first met, on the island there was only one family with that name.

This experience only produced more stories that he just had to write, stories based on that drug-dealing loser and other Bonjours he must have made up, everyone signed by different pen names that never seemed to be the right one. And she, of course, had to read them, praising sections, always suggesting that he simplify but ever careful not to trample his tender dream of becoming a Borges or Cortázar. Two years it took for her to realize her mistake from the start, that reading them only collaborated with her nemesis, and since that insight she refused to read his manuscripts, and he stopped leaving them for her. But her heart remained scarred: he patently loved writing more than he loved her. Her defeat to writing left him owing a debt that accrued high interest over their eight married years, the debt she was now collecting in installments every time she met her younger, graduate-student lover.

Her conviction that she had a compensatory right to this affair, coupled with a certainty that it was an absolute secret, doubled her fortitude to resist any sympathy for Manuel's intuition-provoked jealousy tantrums or any remorse after his exploratory accusations that only succeeded in making her life impossible.

Four days ago he had accused her flat out of infidelity, and she declined to dignify his suspicions by even discussing the matter. She laughed off his ridiculousness, which she described as "his pathetic insecurity," a response that left him even more infuriated. They hadn't spoken since. Then that very morning, on her way out the door, she discovered this manuscript on the dining table. A repulsive, stick-on yellow note thumbed its nose at her from the title page: "I think you will enjoy this one." What brass! After months of his badgering, meanness and insults—and especially now at the rockiest moment of their marriage—he dared to give her the thing she most loathed.

And yet the very shamelessness of his daring also seduced her, titillated her with a sleazy curiosity to see exactly to what depths he was capable of stooping. She had stuffed the manuscript into her briefcase, thinking she might browse through it during her free period at the public high school where she taught Spanish classes, but in the whirlwind day of student problems and faculty meetings, she had forgotten all about it.

Now, half her mind advocated that she discard it, which she almost did before the more curious other half persuaded her to put back *Doña Flora,* move aside the cardboard cup and turn the title page of "Cappuccino."

Evelyn was thoroughly enjoying this first day of a weekend alone, a spring Saturday to herself at an outdoor café in Greenwich Village. Noel had flown down to San Juan at dawn. His father was very ill. She recalled hearing the door close before fading back to sleep. An hour later, she bounced out of bed, energetic, blissfully conscious of Noel's absence, giving her a day with no husband to interrogate her and without the chants of *yo hablo, tú hablas, él habla* by black, Korean, Greek, Italian teenagers. She performed her calisthenics and exercises to Dr. Esteban Echevarren Wilson's Saturday morning health advice on the radio.

She had not failed to work out every morning for over a year, ever since she convinced herself that her excess pounds were the congealed accumulation of her unhappiness. Marshaling her uncommon willpower, she vowed to make herself young again, and this morning, for the first time in ten years, she weighed the same as on the day she married Noel. The pride in her accomplishment made her feel strong, giving her the confidence to now tackle her unhappiness and the clutter in her mind. After showering, she picked out a favorite silk blouse and a old pair of jeans that fit her again. She came to this café to spend an afternoon free of stress, enjoy the cappuccino she had just ordered, and converse on several important matters with her diary.

Manuel's story exhibited his characteristic presumptuousness. The parallels between Evelyn and herself were transparent, and she couldn't believe the fluke of his concocting a character who kept a diary, a secret she never once told him. But wasting any time on this story would only exalt his insufferable arrogance. She looked at her watch: at least a twenty-minute wait. As she drank from the cardboard cup, a warm bread aroma wafted from the mall's bakery, and she craved a piece with jelly. She had resisted the artificial sweetener and now wished she hadn't. Her craving for something sweet distracted her from her indignation at Manuel, and now she would need a stronger distraction from her craving. She reached for *Doña Flora* but, succumbing at the last second to her unquenched curiosity, left it in the briefcase.

Evelyn's diary was her only close and trustworthy friend. It was also her most intimate secret, kept in one of the many stacked shoeboxes in her closet. She would call on it for companionship and carry it for days in her briefcase. Of its existence, Noel surely knew nothing as he paid so little attention to anything important to her. Noel, a lawyer, was consumed by a single passion, his career. He wouldn't even notice that she had awakened transformed and not just in weight. Indifferent to her feelings, he wouldn't imagine her pouring them out on a page.

Exactly what she was anxious to do that day not solely because she felt changed: that night she had dreamed of her first husband. It wasn't a sexual dream. He just came up to her somewhere in the city and said hello. She did ask herself what the scene possibly meant. Noel was the verbalizer, the compulsive theorizer and cross-examiner. She was the simplifier, for whom a discomforting thought was an insect repulsively walking out into her consciousness, begging to be squashed.

Evelyn's cappuccino arrived in a porcelain cup too hot to put to her lips. She flipped through the diary pages, stopping at an entry written sometime before she began her diet. "Blue jeans don't zip, fitted skirts had to be worn with the top button undone, covered over with a sweater. My favorite silk blouses want to pop." The entry was much too depressing. She rapidly turned to the first blank page and positioned the pen, which did not write anything. After carrying around the desire to write something about her dream, she didn't know what to say. She nestled the pen in the inner margins and closed the diary. She raised the still hot porcelain cup using both hands. Savoring her cappuccino, she sat back to observe the passers by along Bleeker and MacDougal.

But the moment was blighted by an inner voice, which forced her to acknowledge that neither the lovely day nor a desire to be alone with her diary had brought her to this particular outdoor café. Enrique lived on MacDougal Street. She chose this café and this table to possibly catch sight of him as he walked from or to the subway. But why should she feel guilty about admitting this to herself? She preferred not to know. To circumvent this dangerous introspection she invoked her gift, a titanium-strong willpower that enabled her to customize her convictions. She wanted to believe that she had come to this café simply for the cappuccino and to be by herself on a lovely afternoon.

After hard concentration, she felt honest in believing exactly as she wanted. Thus unburdened of qualms, she mused whether, happening to be in the neighborhood, she should call Enrique. She took a quarter out of her handbag but unexpectedly slid it under the paper napkin. Why was she holding back? She opened the diary and picked up the pen. "I am sitting in the Village two blocks from Enrique's. I want to call him, but I don't." She added, in English, "Help!" and closed the diary.

In her mind flashed a portrait that made her shudder: the heavy older Evelyn she was on the day she met the new young student-teacher who walked into her classroom looking exactly like her first husband, his swagger, his boyish beardless face, his black hair, his mustache. Enrique was the Hector she had met fifteen years before. Did her intense stare flatter Enrique, provoking his reciprocal gaze that induced something like a rearrangement of every one of her body's cells? Was it all a titillation of his ego? Why else would he have flirted with that overweight woman? Whatever the reason, by the end of the school day she had become impatient with her life. By dinnertime she cried out in her soul for a need to change, be lighter, be free to flirt again. That night, unable to sleep beside the snoring Noel, she relived over and over that day's encounter with Enrique.

Evelyn turned back pages of the diary, to her very first entry on Enrique. "He is ten years younger than I. Am I too old for him? The first time, his eyes didn't look at me, they flared. I must have given him the wrong first impression. The power of his resemblance to Hector had overtaken me . . ."

Her reading of the story was interrupted by the groan of a metal chair being dragged back. Across the table, a silver-haired woman had put down a Styrofoam cup with a tea bag dangling over the rim. She was smiling a "thank you for allowing me to join you" smile. A pair of gold-rimmed glasses hung on pale blue ribbon around her neck. The ribbon matched the color of her eyes. She adjusted the chair, perched the glasses on her nose, then splayed a copy of the *Times* over her part of the table.

This invasion of privacy was truly annoying. Manuel's story had just exposed the outer limits of his cold-blooded vanity. Not with his Hector theory, which only rehashed his harangue that a ghost haunted their marriage: the unforgivable insult was his depicting her in some imagined affair that, even though happening to coincide with the truth, revealed that he harbored for her not one ounce of respect, no trust whatever, and no gratitude for how hard she worked to fulfill her duties as a wife to a man who nightly abandoned her. With that speculation, he had terminally driven his pen into their marriage's comatose heart.

Now, feeling fully justified to be at that table and waiting to pay him back, she was determined to finish reading his cruel, maligning story before exacting a just vindication in the company of her lover. With her forehead docked between a thumb and index finger, the shade of her open hand offered a cove in which she could read in private:

In her diary she had written: "In his cultured accent, burnished from study in Spain, Mexico, and Colombia, Enrique's voice was a streaming song, a mist over my skin, a fragrance that refused to wash off. He could have been, like Hector, a radio announcer."

The next morning they met for breakfast at the diner across the street from their school. She consented to dine with him that Sunday at an Italian restaurant, a date for which she prepared by keeping to a liquid diet for three days. Over a wonderful linguine primavera she discovered that he was an aspiring painter who, like Hector, preferred red wines. "Wine inspires him to paint. He refers to the bottles as his inspirational little friends." By the second week he was begging her to visit his apartment, but she put him off. She told him that she was afraid of rumors that would spread throughout the school. She asked him to wait until his student-teaching assignment ended. In fact, she was too ashamed of her body and hoped that by the end of the term her diet and exercises would show results.

But Enrique pleaded, flattered, charmed until, in a burst of love madness, she agreed to a Sunday afternoon rendezvous. Unable to believe that she was going through with it, she found herself on the subway to Manhattan. But when she found his address, she took one step into the building and panicked. She went home and wrote in her diary: "I opened my coat and saw this fat woman about to remove her clothes and embarrass herself before this beautiful young man."

Monday morning Enrique's hurt stare pierced her deeply. She regretted disappointing him but was too mortified to discuss the matter. They circumvented any conversation about what didn't happen. His student teaching would end the following week, he reminded her. This pained her. She exercised harder, but on his final day she didn't feel ready. Before he left, she made it clear to him that if she hadn't given herself to him it was because she was married, because she had come to her senses.

That was five months ago. Now the woman he had seen in her, under the fat, was finally out of her cellulite cocoon and ached to flutter naked before him. She lifted the paper napkin. The forgotten quarter waited to be deposited in a public phone. She let the napkin fall. Sipping the tepid cappuccino with one hand, she held open the diary with the other, turning the pages with her index finger. No other entries about Enrique, only about Noel. "He doesn't remind me of any other man I have loved. I don't feel anything for him. He's a talker, a litigator, a revealer. He insists there's something important I should be telling him about me. He complains he feels left out of my life. I don't understand his insecurity. He wants us to share everything, my sexual fantasies, my past. He wants my life on display, just like that. He wants to rape my privacy."

The accuracy of so many details—that Enrique was a younger man, the dinner at the Italian restaurant, and now even her very thoughts! Her upward-snapping head attracted the attention of the silver-haired woman, who at first poorly camouflaged her reaction by sipping tea, then looked up cautiously, as if nonverbally requesting permission to offer a suggestion.

Averting the woman's grandmotherly eyes, she dissembled by looking around casually, holding in the fury incited by Manuel's pretentious characterization of her most private feelings. At another table, a little boy and his mother each licked a double-scooped cone. If she couldn't wring Manuel's neck, she wanted a cone, double-scooped. Better still, she needed the therapy of her lover.

Her watch said 4:10. He was late. The silver-haired woman rested the *Times* on the table but did not alight her eyes on its pages. A conversation seemed about to begin. Assuming an inviolable air, the younger woman scanned the page for where she had left off.

Noel embodied a sad detour from the road on which Evelyn knew her life should be traveling. She had confessed this only to her diary: "He was never my kind of man. I don't love him. I don't believe I ever did. I understand now I married him to cover my wound after Hector left me, just like that, for no real reason. Now all my unhappiness comes from Noel, and I can't help hating him." She sipped from the cold porcelain cup. Maybe Noel is not a bad husband, she conceded, but he denied her the passion he gave his work and maybe, she increasingly suspected, other women. Weeknights or weekends, his appointments with clients always came first, and when his majesty had a slot free for her, he always played the same broken record with the lyrics "you are holding something back."

Enrique, on the other hand, gave his passion unquestioningly and devoted all his energy to her, happy with whatever she was willing to give. She turned the diary page. "When Noel started talking of having children, he had come to the end of his rope. I was not enough for him. Enrique spoke of not wanting children, of wanting a life. He said that he didn't need children, just me, selfishly to himself. That's what I love about Enrique, his selfishness, his wanting me selfishly. Everything he said reminded me of Hector, who left me for no reason."

Young and slender beside the selfish Enrique who was really also Hector. That was Evelyn's daydream when she saw, among the crosscurrent of pedestrians along Bleeker, the backs of a couple that had just passed by as she read from her diary. Seeing the man from behind made her caffeinated heart pump faster. The same swagger, the same black hair. And that woman, in jeans and a silk blouse like hers, with hair as long as hers used to be.

As the couple waited to cross Bleeker, the man blocked her view of the woman's face. His hand under the woman's hair clutched the nape of her neck, exactly as Hector sometimes did. Evelyn stretched forward to see his face. But with his head turned away, and looking down at the shorter woman, she could not get a look. The pair crossed Bleeker and disappeared down MacDougal—but could he have been Enrique?

That possibility she couldn't bear to consider. That man couldn't be Enrique. He had to be someone else, another Hector in his youth in love with another Evelyn. She invoked her gifted will power, squeezing her eyes shut then opening them to write: "Today in Greenwich Village I saw Hector. It was Hector I saw. There's no doubt in my mind. He's dating a much younger woman." But this time her gift failed. She still suspected the man she saw was Enrique. She closed her eyes again, concentrated very hard. When she opened them, she wrote, "Hector is dating a replica of me. Poor guy, I would say he hasn't gotten over me."

She sat back, took a deep breath, sipped the last icy drops from the cardboard cup. Manuel's arrogance had corroded a wide hole through her tolerance, a hole that would never be patched. Her death-ray stare drilled his visualized face with such ferocity that the woman reading the *Times* raised her head as if she had heard a sound. Her gold-framed eyes looked directly at hers and exuded sympathy, a willingness to get herself involved.

Manuel's manuscript provided the only refuge, but the last paragraph she had read was followed by a half page of white space, ending abruptly. Instead of lifting her head, she kept her eyes riveted to the page as if staring at Manuel himself because this convoluted story was so much like him, layers of complexity and self-serving psychological analyses. That's why she would always prefer the simplicity of a lover to a husband. She was relishing the cleverness of that observation when her thumb unintentionally lifted the story's ostensibly final page, uncovering another one. On this page, the last sentence she had read was followed by an appended, final paragraph.

Evelyn triumphantly closed the diary. Only then did she notice the man standing on the sidewalk, contemplating her. Everything was happening as in her dream. The spontaneous surrender in her eyes watered the flowering of his smile. As he walked around to the entrance in the railing that defined the outdoor table area, she shut her diary and covered it with her purse. Before he reached her table, his eyes were telegraphing the essence of his first words, "You look magnificent. You haven't changed in fifteen years."

"*¿Es tan interesante?* Is it that interesting?"

Was she imagining a voice that she had not heard in years? A man was sitting in the woman's chair.

"What's wrong? It's me."

She blinked, shook her head. "Oh, nothing, nothing's wrong." He held out a long-stemmed rose wrapped in cellophane. Her fingers caressed the cellophane-covered petals. "You're unique, special," she told him. She leaned over and kissed him.

"So what are you reading that left you so lost?" He laid on the table a spiral notebook under volume two of *Don Quixote* and pulled back the chair.

"Oh, some dreary report. My mind drifted to something else. Nothing important, really. But you're so late and now I'm hungry," her widely opened eyelids playing on the ambiguity of "hungry." On top of the manuscript she placed her purse, opened it and plucked out a lipstick case and a small mirror. Over her globe-rounded lips she applied north and south hemispheres of red. They agreed that a pizza and a bottle of red wine at his place would be perfect. She got on her feet, moved the briefcase to her chair and, while putting on her coat, asked how his day had been.

"Nothing much, my Wednesday class . . ."

Listening and nodding, she turned her back to him for a second, during which, in the shadow of her open coat, she lifted the flap of her briefcase and slipped in Manuel's story, folded lengthwise, between a Spanish textbook and the secret compartment where she kept her diary.

Zaxxon

"Making it to Zaxxon's the hardest, then he always shoots you down," Milly explained as she piloted the little video-game jet on the TV screen. "Danny Watanabe made it twice. He says Zaxxon's this big robot with heat-senseless missiles. Um, I don't know what that is, but he says they follow you around till they get you." She wore her new, teen-style outfit—faded jeans, Micky Mouse sweatshirt and ankle-high sneakers—which she had wanted very much to show her Papi, who had to cancel his turn to be with her on Sunday. "Oh, no!" Her jet, after destroying countless silo-launched rockets and after issuing inexhaustible bombs and automatic fire at enemy jets, had exploded in a white splat.

"See how you do it, Mami? Mami? Hello-o-o? Is anybody home?"

"Oh, I'm sorry."

"Are you ready to play with me? And you promised me popcorn."

"I don't know if I understand the game yet. Maybe I should just make the popcorn." "No, later, let me show you how to play." As behind her in the window, half the bedroom away, storm clouds bombarded the window pane with raindrops, Milly illustrated with outstretched thumb and pinky wings how to dodge missiles, played by the other hand's ascending fingers, and how to drop bombs.

Clara listened, recalling how as students she and Alberto spoke just as easily of planting bombs, the only response they could see to the Yankees' violence on their culture. "But, *mi linda,* all you do is blow things up? Don't you have other games to play on this video set? Is this the game that your cousin Carlos left here the other day? I don't like your playing this game."

"But I *like* this game, Mami. All my friends in school play it. It's not just blowing things up. You get points, but we never count them."

"Then what?"

"You keep playing as long as you can to see if you can get to Zaxxon. You get three jets."

"And what does Zaxxon do?"

"I already told you. He's the big robot with missiles that follow the jet, and it's almost impossible to fly away from them. We play to see if we can beat Zaxxon. Gary Vega said he did one time, but we don't believe him. Mami, didn't you play games like this when you were a kid?"

In the window, the storm became darker, angrier. A boom of thunder caused Milly to drop the joystick, trembling as the little girl Clara herself did when tropical storms made her imagine that the sky was cracking into boulders that would fall on her. But now she was the mother into whose arms her girl ran. As outside the lightning and thunder phased out grumbling, Clara hugged tightly, stroking Milly's curly, kissable hair that reflected the TV screen's video colors. Disappointed that she couldn't see her father and now housebound by the rain, who was to tell her to turn off this horrible game, as Clara would have preferred?

"Now, let's play." Milly squeezed a button on the video game master unit, and the TV screen crackled, going black. The "Zaxxon" logo appeared, then a video night sky over an unmoving yellow and green planet. "Move the stick forward, Mami."

"Where's the jet?"

Containing her impatience to rolling her eyes upward, Milly put her index finger under the jet suspended in the screen's lower left corner. Clara's moving the joystick thrust the jet jerkily forward. A purring rose and descended with the jet, which now headed toward a brick wall with a narrow rectangular opening. Milly excitedly instructed her mother to pull the stick back, elevate the jet into the rectangular opening of the floating brick wall into which it crashed because Clara's mind was really on Alberto.

He was due to call again soon, determined to penetrate her resistance and continue to carry out the litigation he had started, encouraged by Milly's campaign that the three of them live as a family again. Just that morning Milly asked that her next birthday present be that she allow Papi to come back. *"No, it's not the storm. There's no storm here in Atlanta, Clara, but I have to stay because the prosecution came up with a surprise motion. We have to change our strategy for Monday's session."* Alberto was defending one of four urban guerrillas on trial for planting bombs to bring about Puerto Rico's independence, their great cause that always came first. His sigh of exhaustion blew heavily into the mouthpiece. The federal prosecutors had broken so many laws to hang his client, he vented, as if expecting her sympathy, forgetting that she was no longer his wife, that their struggle was now his to face alone.

"See, if you make it past the first jets, then these smaller robots, Zaxxon's slaves, come after you. They shoot regular missiles. You can fly over them, like this." Milly dodged the rockets and continued bombarding silos, magazines, airplane hangars before nosing toward a rectangular field of squiggly radiation waves. The jet gracefully arched over the danger and Clara applauded, taxing Milly's concentration, causing her to succumb to an oncoming squadron of enemy jets.

It was Clara's turn again. Her second plane took off, once more approaching the brick wall with the rectangular gap. Her jittery hand jerked the joystick and, out of sheer luck, guided the jet through the gap. Meanwhile, in the video sky, from underground silos rose staggered rockets that almost hit the zigzagging jet that escaped but without attacking, wreaking no damage on vulnerable hangars and magazines because she couldn't both dodge and press the firing button at the joystick's base. Up ahead approached the radiation field. The jet dipped when it should have soared and was radioactively fried.

"You're supposed to attack too," Milly reminded her.

Her *marriage* had been a counterattack, performed in a decade when the worldwide Revolution was at hand, and just beyond her generation's grasp awaited their own pinnacle of "justice" and "liberation," their own socialist island republic. To be prepared for it, within two months of graduating from City College she and Alberto married, but in their minds untraditionally, as revolutionary, egalitarian partners, as *compañeros*. This political commitment, this progressive consciousness from a man from her own culture—and not like those Rican sisters who dreamed of surrendering themselves to some *gringo*—was to be her salvation.

The grand nephew of the fiery nationalist Justo Bonjour, Alberto was never liked by her parents. Her father staunchly defended Puerto Rico's permanent union with the *americanos,* even though he returned from Korea complaining of racist fellow soldiers who tormented him and who, he suspected, were capable of killing him with friendly fire. But he hated Communism more and saw the nationalists as Moscow's dupes who wanted to entrap his island with lies and false dreams as happened to Cuba. On the other hand, her mother didn't really care about Alberto's politics. Her problem with him was that he was a Bonjour, which should have forewarned Clara that she was going to be miserable.

Clara, of course, didn't listen to old island talk. She knew the difference between the men of those times and the "New" man that a revolutionary consciousness produces. Alberto treated women as equals. That's why she didn't listen to her parents' pleas to stop thinking foolishness: she forsook graduate school to teach, to earn a salary that could help Alberto through law school so he could work to bring justice to their people and free the island. But her later suspicion that he was involved with another revolutionary *compañera* prompted the waning of her own commitment, her tripping into the traditional wife's jealousies and backsliding into the concession that her mother's reactionary generation was right about everything.

"You did pretty good, Mami." The phone rang.

"Answer it, honey. I'm going to make popcorn." From the kitchen, every noise she made—the clanging of the pot carefully removed from stacked pots, the gas range's bloom of blue flames, the sizzling oil and butter, the grating sound of kernels raining into the pot—fragmented her unintentional eavesdropping. *"Political changes don't happen in one final encounter, and other things are also as important. I realize that now."* That was how he began his summation to the jury in her heart that morning, not allowing her to cut him off until he concluded, *"I know you won't believe me, but it really hurts to have to cancel my day with Milly. Look, I'm coming to the end of a chapter in my life. I know I screwed up everything by giving more attention to other things than to us. So what I want is a chance to prove . . ."* But he could not continue because he had to get to court, offering relief for Clara, who for the first time since their divorce almost allowed herself to hear his sincerity.

On hanging up, she also immediately knew that his change came too late. Her life was stable now, rooted in the present, in struggling for Milly and in defining a sharper sense of herself. That was her pledge of allegiance to her new life, however grudging. She had to find another way to save Milly from the stupid, corrosive self-doubts that this ridiculous gringo culture will plant in her heart to sap her life's energy. Milly will not grow up in the dignity of their Spanish-speaking paradise in a perfect, Marxist future, but Clara didn't want her informed by the oppressively silly American conversation. Alberto's call had stirred up that old anger.

"Look at that pathetic Bonjour that they found dead in a motel. That he had my last name, my blood, made me angry. My cousin Manuel, the reporter, looked into that guy's story to see if he came from our part of the Bonjours. He didn't. He was an assimilated guy, a pathetic guy. God knows what he was looking for back in his old neighborhood. I think he was probably a police informant and got caught. But he's an example of what I didn't want for Milly, a person with no identity, just a constant life of trying to prove to these pretentious people that she is good enough or looking for forgiveness for being what she is in the arms of her oppressor. That's why I devoted all my energy . . ."

He talked fast. He had sensed her weakening and didn't let her go until he was called to handle trial matters. She knew him enough to know that he would be relentless, so she wasn't going to talk to him again until she gathered her strength and reinforcements.

"Mami, its Papi . . ."

"I'm making popcorn right now and it'll burn," she answered, just as the potted tempest ended.

Milly, appearing not to have heard, came into the kitchen. "Papi wants to talk to you."

"Tell him to call back later. I'm busy right now." Milly gave the original message about the popcorn and to call later.

Clara entered the bedroom bearing a large bowl. Milly gladly put down her joystick to have the bowl on her lap. "Papi said that he'll probably be too busy to call until dinnertime." Clara watched her eat one grain at a time, her way of savoring and prolonging the pleasure. She pointed to the joystick. "Now you, Mami." In the window, a huge flash before a rumble shook the building. Milly's hand twitched, propelling some of the popcorn out of the bowl. She looked at the floor, then at her mother. "Don't worry, I'll clean it up." Another roll of thunder. Milly stood, looking anxious. Clara put the bowl on the floor and hugged her, absorbed Milly's fear. She whispered into Milly's ear: "If the telephone rings I think we shouldn't answer it. I want us to play without interruptions. Maybe we can come face to face with Zaxxon. I think I'm ready for him."

"What if it's Papi."

"Didn't you tell me that he was going to be busy until dinner time? And look, it's a little after two now. Anyway, the answering machine can take it and we'll hear if it's him."

"Okay, let's start again. Just us. I'll go first." As if Milly's resetting the game had also switched off the daylight, the afternoon suddenly went dark. Clara turned on the night-table lamp. By that lamp she had waited in bed for Alberto's late call until she gave up and went to sleep. Milly picked up the joystick and proceeded to pilot, squaring off against the first minion robot. A red missile sizzled from the robot's chest. It sailed above and past the skillfully swooping jet. "Milly, that was terrific." She flew through wall gaps and electronic barriers, laying waste missile silos, knocking out every minion robot and enemy squadron, the whole obstacle range three times while still working on her first jet. The phone began to ring.

Milly suspended the game to hear who was calling. *Ring.* Before the answering machine awoke, Clara left the room to get the broom and dust pan to clean up the popcorn scattered on the bedroom floor. *Ring.* The ringing pursued her into the kitchen, drilling the air, locked into her heat until interrupted by the answering machine that amplified Alberto's voice. Milly picked up, and Clara paused in the kitchen to overhear Milly speaking to her father. Waiting for Milly to tell her to pick up in the kitchen, she honed her determination to cut him off and even counterattack his appeals—shot out of silos, swarming in squadrons—that she take him back. She had survived weeks of this game, losing ground every time, to arrive at what felt more and more like this, the decisive moment. But unlike the little jet programmed to battle without exhaustion, she suddenly lacked the desire to engage in another confrontation because—it occurred to her at that very second—no matter what he said, everything he asked came down to defining who she was and what she wanted for herself right now. And what was that? Who was she now?

Not the liberated, Anglo-free *puertorriqueña* she had dreamed of in the seventies. That person will never exist. But who has taken her place? And what else mattered now beside watching Milly grow up lonely for a father and seeing herself growing older alone? And what "Clara" did Alberto think he wanted to have again as his *compañera*? Will he accept the "Puerto Rican–American minority person" she must resign herself to being?

She waited for Milly, who never called her and instead continued her game.

"Mami, come, I think I'm going to make it to Zaxxon. Papi said he'll call right back."

Ominously introduced by a nasal digitized music, a king-sized version of the minion robots ploddingly advanced from the right-hand edge of the screen. Zaxxon shot a missile and Milly's jet survived it. As Milly played, absorbed in her game, Clara thought of pressing the off button on the answering machine and turning off the phone's ringer but immediately remembered the effort would be pointless. Even if she turned off the answering machine, the phone would continue to ring because the ringer button had stopped working the night that, to dramatize her request to know why Alberto couldn't make a simple call, she threw the phone crashing on the night table.

Milly sighed an "Ay" of disappointment when Zaxxon finished off her valiant jet. "Mami, you see like I told you? Zaxxon always gets you."

Clara visualized herself suspended like the little jet in a night void in which instead of ominous, digitized sound she heard Milly's voice pleading for her father while looming enormous and aiming its unfailing missiles was her realization that Alberto wasn't her Zaxxon. She was.

The Ride

The Palm Tree Beach Shop wasn't on the business strip a block ahead, where it should have been, but unexpectedly on this residential street. Luckily I saw the big Palm Tree sign in time to brake, back up my van, and park beside a beat-up VW bug in front of the store's glass door. Just when I pulled in, from behind the shop's door a man in his early thirties waved, then picked up an attaché case and put on his sunglasses before coming out into the sun. He was a mustached blond guy, dressed in a white knit shirt, pants and deck shoes, looking like a resplendent cruise ship captain. He pulled open the passenger door, allowing in the noon furnace heat, and climbed into the van, hand outstretched, "Hi, I'm Rob."

"Julián had to pick up a stranded motor scooter. He'll meet us at the pier. I'm one of his older brothers, Frank."

"Well, it's my pleasure." Rob's thin, peaking mustache flattened above his piano-keys smile. He slid the attaché case between his legs. The leather case was embossed with Aztec designs.

I started backing up. "Nice case."

"My wife's gift. It's Mexican. The designs are Aztec."

I veered to make a right at the light, thinking of avoiding the noontime congestion on Baldroity. I signaled to make another right at Calle Júpiter and then cut through Ocean Park. "Why don't you turn right on Jupiter, then go through Ocean Park? Yeah, at this light, then at the next one up ahead. "

I asked how long he had been living on the island.

"Fifteen years. Turn left here before you get to the beach road where the kids always double-park. Over there, left down there by that tall white building." I thought it humorous that this younger man thought he should conduct my driving through streets I knew before he was born. "Here, left here." We turned left. "So, Frank, why does your brother want to sell his business?"

"I thought he only wants to sell half."

"That's what I meant."

"I think he needs working capital to expand. He said a friend recommended you."

"Yeah, a Brazilian guy who sells me bikinis. You work for Julián full-time?"

Our eyes met briefly, "I'm just here visiting. I live in—"

Rob rolled down his window and shouted out, "Hernández!," waving at a powder blue suit standing in conversation with a dark blue suit. In the rearview mirror, the powder blue suit waved back. Rob rolled up the window. "I asked business friends about Julián."

"I'm surprised that you haven't come around to meet him before and talk over business."

"Well, I'm working at the shop most of the time. I only recently saw this scooter business by the pier. I came around a couple of times but for some reason he was never there. I asked the cop at the pier who told me that once he rents out the scooters, he takes off somewhere."

"He probably goes to a café and sits with friends. Once the scooters are gone they don't come back for the rest of the day. The point of life is enjoying it, don't you think?"

"Yeah, I agree with that, but not during working hours. I'm surprised because I was told that Julián lived for many years in New York."

"He did."

"Had a pretty distinct accent on the phone."

"Yeah, strange, he has that, too. But it comes and goes. It's weird, you know."

"Man, I couldn't live in *los Nuevayores*. Hate it. Eats you up."

"I know. I recently heard about a second cousin of ours, we were distant, and I never even met him, and he never had anything to do with my family. Anyway, it appears that he started out okay, studied, had a profession, then got involved with some drug dealers and got killed. It was in the newspapers."

"Ugly news indeed. And this place has changed for the worse. I think it's the influence of Newyoricans too."

"You been held up?"

"Once, just once. The second time I was packing a gun. Blew the sucker away. That's what you got to do, man. They don't mess with you after that. Word gets around."

We were passing the hotels on Ashford. A taxi ahead of us stopped to let out a fare. Clouds doused the sun. A dark-skinned, white-haired, seersuckered man stepped out of the cab, then held out his hand to a blond in a gray business suit, skirt well above her knees.

"Right on, Gilberto!" He started to roll down the window but stopped. "Better not." His index finger pointed. "See that guy? Speaker of the House, good friend of mine."

"Must be on his lunch hour."

"Yeah, Gilberto's no vegetarian."

The taxi ahead was trapped behind a bus that in turn was obstructed and honking. We enjoyed the blond's gait as she strode to the hotel entrance. I knew her from a few years back, when she worked at the telephone company and used to have lunch with her girlfriends in a little diner I owned the last time I moved down from New York. We went out a few times until my wife found out. We were practically separated, but she got so jealous she started showing up at the diner until we got together again. The car behind me honked to tell me that the taxi had finally taken off.

"So why are you interested in the motor scooter business?"

"Well, I have a few businesses around. I rent out sailboats on Vieques, produce rock concerts. I just think your brother's business is a good investment. He's got that place by the pier, in front of the cruise ships." He flashed his movie star smile.

"Did you get in trouble when you shot that guy?"

"Oh that, nothing happened. Didn't kill him, and besides I know some pretty important people here." Smile. "You look like you spent a long time in the States, so you know how crazy things work down here. If I wanted I could probably become mayor of at least three towns." Smile. The sun came out again. We had crossed the Dos Hermanos bridge and were heading toward the colonial part of the city. "Do you work for Julián, Frank?"

"I live in New York. I'm just spending the summer here. I'm between jobs, you could say. I used to work for a trucking company. I just went through a divorce, so I'm helping Julián out and getting to know the business."

"Hate New York. Hate working with stress—or working for anybody. I prefer this. Sunshine, branching out all the time. My own boss."

. . . That's the advantage of having your own business, Frank, even if it lacks the prestige of finishing two years of night-school college. In your friends' eyes, I am a failure because I didn't have any college like you. I'm sure everybody advised: Don't listen to the loser Julián. But renting motor scooters is a good business, Frank, think of it now that you lost your job. Just see what we can do with this business, make it grow—it's a decent change of careers for anybody. I may not know a lot, but I was right about your snobby wife who didn't want you because you were still just an office manager and not some high executive and treated you cold, who when she found out that you had another woman, one who gave you what warmth she denied you . . . blamed your Bonjour blood . . .

A trailer truck backing into a dockside warehouse held up traffic in both directions. "So it's the spot in front of the pier that you really want?"

"Oh, yeah, that's where the cruise passengers pass through the gates. His scooters are the first thing they see. That's a prime spot for anything. I know how we can make the most of it. But he's the only business with the license to it. I don't know how he managed it, but it was a sharp move, brilliant in fact. It's mostly the place, that's why I want to buy in, for the location. He'll understand that. We can both benefit."

Something happened to the truck backing in. A man came out of the warehouse to talk to the driver. He pointed inside the warehouse.

"This shit always happens. You know what that's all about? It's a sunken street drain on the other side of the truck. These guys have to move another truck inside the warehouse so this one can get in at a weird angle. The trucks can't just straighten out and pull in, so they create this jam."

"So why are you settling for only half Julián's business? Why don't you make him an offer for the whole thing?"

"That's all Julián's willing to sell. Typical island shit, that hole's been there almost a month."

. . . I know, Frank, what you probably said to yourself when I gave up on New York and came back to San Juan: "The island is okay for Julián because he belonged among those hicks and their ass-backward ways, on that island of slow people, where everything runs late or breaks down. He still calls himself Bonjour."

Besieged by honking cars, the truck finally backed into the warehouse. Now cars in both directions had to alternate using the only level side of the road. After that, it was minutes to the pier, which was quiet, with no cruise ships due in until tomorrow. At the gate the only person around was the pier policeman, López, who chatted with a woman shading herself with an umbrella. López was incapable of letting a woman escape his attention. He used to live right off St. Mary's Park in the Bronx, right around the corner where my ex-wife went to live with my son Gabriel when he was a kid. I always wished that López would find himself another job. Seeing him always made me think about that central failure in my life.

I parked the van so Rob could get a good look at the new scooters chained together. Behind them, the skinny old wino Samuel, who lived in the park behind the scooters, was stretched out on a bench, having nodded off in the shade of the overhanging almond tree. Rob stepped out of the van and looked around. No Julián. He took a notepad out of his shirt pocket and, from different points, counted paces, then paused to write. He looked over the chained row of motor scooters and jotted something down. When he finished he returned the pad to his pocket and went over to Samuel on the bench. *"Oye, ¿adónde se fue el dueño?* Hey, where's the owner?"

Samuel sat up startled.

"Oye, el dueño, Julián Bonjour ¿dónde está? The owner, Julián Bonjour, where is he?" Samuel looked around confused. He pointed to the van.

Rob walked back shaking his head. "He's telling me this is Julián's van. He don't know shit."

"It's lunch hour. Maybe Julián went home for lunch. That's what he normally does."

"But he sent you to pick me up, for Christ's sake, to talk business. Where was that scooter stranded?"

"That was just up here by the El Morro fortress. He must have gotten back and figured we got stuck in traffic, so he went to have lunch. Let's get something to eat. He'll probably return by the time we get back. You know how things work around here."

Rob returned to the van, shut the door. *"Hombre,* funny way of doing business."

"Renting, I'm finding out, is a funny business. I've watched Julián closely. He depends on eye contact, how he feels about somebody." . . . *Julián knew. No college courses, no uppity wife, no executive career training, but he knew some things* . . .

"I know, but I would need to see some changes. My Brazilian friend tells me Julián doesn't rent to some people if he doesn't trust their looks. And if he likes them he lets them pay with a check. I couldn't live with that. Strictly credit cards. None of his hocus pocus."

"I used to think the same thing at first, but I realized that cards might eliminate some of your business."

"Local business, which is pretty risky already."

"Locals fill the dead time when the ships don't bring tourists."

We pulled into El Hamburger, which overlooked the Atlantic. The daily epic sunlight, the whiteness and size of the clouds over the blue and turquoise ocean, the old Spanish fortifications jutting out against the balmy sky, was a sight never less than spectacular. At the El Hamburger, the only free table was against a back wall. The lunch crowd was mostly government employees from the Capitol building nearby. Rob surveyed the place as if for somebody he knew. We ordered two burgers and beers. "So, do you want to be a mayor?"

"Naw, I'd just like the clout. For instance, I'm having a zoning problem back at the store. City's always been trying to close me up. I'm really in a residential area."

"How do you get around the marshals?"

Great big smile, pleased I asked. "People I know, but there's always somebody else who wants a cut. You know how it is here." He talked and looked around. The beers arrived fast.

"Rob, where are you from originally?"

"New Orleans." He sipped from the frosted beer stein.

"How'd you get here?"

"My wife's parents. Connecticut Yankees with a business here. We came down on vacation . . ."

. . . Your wife envisioned a lifetime island vacation until she learned how much you hated the idea. So you didn't have to come down to please her, and you were going nowhere where you were working, and her feelings for you dried up with her dreams of living in a tropical paradise. Then the most intelligent one, the one who thought himself better than his brothers, became so tormented at home that he lost his job and landed in the arms of another woman . . .

"I got into the scene right away, began to see things the locals were blind to. You know that grassy cliff across the avenue here, looking out at the ocean? I saw it was a perfect place for a rock concert. Got a permit. Convinced Pepsi to sponsor it. It was a smash." Big, big smile.

. . . So he tells his sad story to his older, always-hustling brother Julián, who got the idea: Frank, don't be afraid to come back. You were born here. You can't change what you are, where you came from. Help me build this rental business, scooters now, cars later. Apply whatever you learned in your experience to my business . . . But this offer was a painful blow to the ego. The "different" brother took a long time to even call back and say hello . . .

"Did the same thing down in Ponce. Another smash concert. Then my in-laws gave us the house where the store is. It was a residence, so opening a business was really illegal, but since it was only a block from the business area, I took a chance. Broke down some walls and built the store."

The burgers came as Rob was in the middle of his second speech on how thieves should be blown away. Our eating left a lull.

"Rob, what's wrong with your car that you couldn't drive?"

"Oh, it's that old Volky you saw in front of my store."

"That rusty bug?"

"It still runs. I have a guy who was supposed to come in and work on it—an illegal Dominican. He owes me a favor. But he didn't show. You know the story."

"Why don't you get yourself a newer car?"

"Na, this one's okay for my needs. I got it from some guy who owed me a favor. I figure somebody else will give me the next car." He looked at his watch. "Do you think Julián's back by now? I can't deal with this laid-back island way of running things."

We finished eating, paid the tab and were soon in the van, rolling down the steep street to the pier.

. . . Your call from New York did come, Frank, after you realized you couldn't go back to the island, that you didn't think you "could hack that place, take that step." Down, of course, was what you meant . . .

At the traffic light, I turned and passed the pier gate and the motor scooters, continuing in the direction of Rob's Palm Tree Shop. López waved, and I glanced at him receding in the mirror.

"Hey, where we going?"

"I told you I was helping Julián out. I know him like I know myself. I don't think this deal will be good for him."

Rob briefly lost his bearings, but quickly regained them and chuckled to himself, complete with Baby Grand grin. At the next light I smiled at Rob. Thumb cocked, he aimed an index-finger muzzle and fired: "Julián, I like your style."

PC

Now that I got my own Personal Computer, I'm the happiest kid in the world. I wanted one since last year when I started to go really nuts about the PCs at St. Barnabas. Brother Sylvester was the first teacher to learn how to use them, and I was in his advanced eighth-grade class because of my hundreds in math. Our term project was to write a program, a game that's like a story with logical questions, but I couldn't finish mine before summer because we only had four PCs for about twenty kids, and nobody had one at home because they cost too much. Sly got ours at school donated from an electronics store. They were demos, the old kind with green monitors only for letters and numbers, so they don't run video games. Sly the Fly said he liked the way my program was going and he would give me a good grade if I finished it. But I couldn't because of everything that happened. Now with my own PC maybe I can finish it. But I don't know if I'll be going back to St. B's because maybe Luisa is going to send me to my family in Puerto Rico.

Before the school got those PCs I used to only think about girls and sex. I never had a girl, but this big black kid in my class, Henry Bell, was doing it with this white woman, thirty-five, and used to tell us about it. He showed pictures of her, naked with her legs wide open and her face grinning between them and at the camera. When he showed that picture in the gym the guys went nuts. The girl I want to see naked is Leticia, who lives in the building directly across from mine, on the second floor too. She has big tits, and I always used to look out my window to see when she comes home from high school or if she's at her window. But that was before I joined the Computer Club and got home too late to see her.

In school we write programs in BASIC. That's a high-level language, which means like a language with human numbers and ABCs. BASIC language translates ABCs into the language that the computer uses, its deeper thinking part. I'll learn some of that maybe in the Bronx High School of Science where I want to go. Brother Sly calls writing a program talking to the computer, but I don't think it's talking. It's putting your words directly into its mind, a kind of mental telepathy, like creatures do from outer space. When I enter my program, the computer daydreams when it's just me writing stuff into its memory.

I used to live alone with my aunt Luisa. She sewed downtown at a factory. She always came home at six. When I was like in the fourth and fifth grade Doña Conchita downstairs used to take care of me until Luisa gave me my own key. I had to be home before it got dark. I used to just go home and maybe hang out on the stoop for a while with some of the kids on the block. That was before I joined the Computer Club. When Luisa was working I was alone because my big sister's away in school in PR so she doesn't grow up in this neighborhood. My mother is away too because she's very sick.

When I was a little kid I thought I wanted to be a priest because the brothers in school always talked about heaven. I thought heaven was the greatest thing because of how beautiful everything looked in the paintings in church, especially the one on the roof over the altar. It has these big fluffy clouds, with the saints and the angels like body surfing on them. I used to go to sleep dreaming of me and my family at the beach in heaven forever. Heaven sounds pretty cool. In religion class Brother Dimas told us that in heaven you just think of a place and you're there. Souls don't even have to talk. They read each other's thoughts. I really liked that. In heaven is where Luisa always jokes that I will see Papi again, when God arrests him for not paying child support. She says God keeps a special place for all the Bonjour fathers.

My PC is better than the one we had in school. They were older ones with 5" floppy drives. The slot for the disk looked like a mouth with a very thin smile. Sly's computer had a hard drive and a color monitor that was great for the kind of games he wouldn't let us play. Games like Pac-Man and Frogger. He only let us play adventure games, the kind you have to read. That's the kind we program, like writing a story but with choices. You're the hero of the story, and you decide where to move and how many weapons and shields you take with you. Usually there's an evil master who seems to be able to do anything and knows everything. He has the kingdom enslaved. He can only be stopped by some crystal or a special ring or something. And once he's dead you become the hero of the land. My program is like that. It's called Evil Wizard.

Brother Sly was helping me with it, but it takes a long time to write it without bugs, and we had to be out of the school by five. That's why I wanted Luisa to get me a PC, even just an old one with a green monitor, so I would have something to do now that she had stopped getting home at six. But she always said they were too expensive. I told her that maybe if my mother got some money and helped out, then I could get one for Christmas or my birthday. She yelled at me in Spanish that my mother was sick and where would she get the money. Another day I kind of mentioned it again and about Mami helping out, and she blew up again. Why couldn't I get things through my thick head that I shouldn't bother her with the computer.

So I didn't get a computer that time. She also said I couldn't hang out on the stoop downstairs. I should come home and do my homework and watch TV. I really didn't care that much now that my best friend Martin had stopped hanging out. Sometimes I saw him from the window. He mostly came home when it was dark. Somebody usually drove him in a Caddy or a Mercedes. He had started wearing really nice clothes and was usually with some really sexy fox. He used to go to St. B's but got kicked out because he started playing hooky. One day Luisa just said she didn't want to see me with him.

In my game a good wizard welcomes you to the game and asks your name. My name is Philip so I type P-H-I-L-I-P and enter.

Then you are asked how many family members you have. You choose a number from two to ten. The more family you have, the harder the game gets. The good wizard then tells you the story of the game. Brother Sly touched it up and corrected it for grammar. This is how it starts: *In a far away land an evil wizard keeps your family hostage. For each he demands 100 gold pieces in ransom. You have been searching for your family for many weeks. The wizard has sent you a note informing you that he has your family in his castle and telling you about the ransom. You bring with you 100 gold pieces for every member of your family.* There's more. The evil wizard keeps your family invisible in his castle. You're given enough gold coins when you start out, but the wizard has goons that steal coins from you, and then you have to win them back by tossing dice. And even if you free your entire family, you also have to win enough coins to rescue yourself.

Brother Sly helped me with the part about choosing the number of hostages to make the game easier or harder. And it was his idea to use the gold pieces. Then he asked me a lot of questions about parts that didn't work which I had to change. He was teaching me how to write the goon part and the dice game. They're called subroutines. Those are pieces of program that get used over and over. He said if I finish the game he would enter it in a student science contest. He said it might even help me get into the Bronx High School of Science. He said I deserve to make it there because it took me a long time to figure out this game. I started others and stopped working on them. I had just got to writing the selection of the rooms when summer vacation started.

Martin has big muscles. He used to be my best friend. I look really skinny next to him. I remember when he first got his weights. We were in the sixth grade. That's all he did. Pump iron. He was going to be left back. Didn't do his homework or nothing else, just his weights. He got these big muscles and became like my big brother and my bodyguard. Nobody messed with me because of him. His grandma Doña Conchita used to take care of me so when I stayed there we were always together. Last summer I went to stay with my sister in my older aunt Dalia's house in PR, and when I came back Luisa said I won't be staying at Dona Conchita's no more. It cost too much Luisa said, and besides I was already big enough to stay home by myself.

That night Aunt Dalia called from PR. Whatever Dalia said surprised Luisa, who hung up promising to call back. I was watching TV and asked what had happened, and she said it had nothing to do with me. I asked her where she was going, but she didn't answer. She had gone to the super's house downstairs and came up with the *Daily News*. I asked her again what's going on. She said she wanted to see what movies were playing. I told her that Brother Sly had brought the same paper to class and asked me if I had a death in my family. Luisa looked at me for a long time.

Later that night, when she thought I was asleep, she called Dalia back. I heard her tell Dalia that she had read about it. Dalia talked more until Luisa said she didn't know who that guy was, but knowing my father and his being a Bonjour, she wouldn't be surprised if one day she read a similar story about him. She read from the newspaper to Dalia. The report said that he wasn't the kind of person you would think was mixed up with drugs. Dalia said something for a long time; then Luisa said that if that dead guy lived pretty good in Riverdale, then he didn't sound like a Bonjour from my father's branch. Then Dalia said something for a long time again, and this time Luisa answered "Oh" and "Really" and then "My God." Dalia was still talking when I fell asleep.

I couldn't find that newspaper the next day. She must have returned it. Another strange thing was that it was Saturday, and Luisa went out in the middle of the day. She had never done that before. Some man called; then she got dressed up. She looked pretty. She smelled nice, too. I asked her where she was going, and she said just out to lunch. I asked her who the guy was, but she said we would talk about that later. A car was honking downstairs. I looked out the window and saw the car. It was a red Buick, wow, brand new. I asked her who the guy was again, and she said it was a friend of hers. She left me some money to go see a movie and showed me some food she left prepared in the fridge. She planned to be back after dinner. I went to see *Star Wars* for the fourth time. When I got back Luisa was already home, and she was sitting on the sofa crying. Dalia called from PR. It was about my sister. She ran away with a man. She was only fifteen. He could have been her father, Luisa said. Nobody knew where she was. I wondered if she was kidnapped. Maybe she could be ransomed like in my game. I thought about this all that night and about my mom.

She lived in Manhattan, but Luisa says she couldn't live with us because she was sick. She came to the Bronx to see me a couple of times, and I noticed that her hands were like red balls. The last time she came she wanted to kiss me, and I didn't let her because her breath smelled bad and she looked very sick. The night my sister ran away with that man I went to bed thinking about my mother and how I didn't kiss her the last time. My aunt woke me up and asked me what was wrong. I asked her about what. I said I was dreaming of my sister, which I was, and my mother too, but I remembered not to mention my mother to my aunt. She said that I was making noises and woke her up. She brought a towel because I was all wet with sweat.

Mami must have read my mind, because the next day Luisa and me had just come back from mass, and she was waiting for us downstairs. Her hair was short like a kid's and dyed a white blond, which looked really funny. She was wearing a man's leather jacket that covered her hands except for the tips of her fingers. My aunt just told her to go away. She said she came to see me because she missed me. Luisa grabbed my hand and told me to keep walking. Mami followed us up the stairs. Her fat red hand kept stroking the back of my head. Inside the apartment Luisa told her she can stay a little while. Luisa gave her a cup of coffee then went into the bedroom. Mami mixed in about ten teaspoons of sugar. She asked me about school and about my friends. I almost asked her if she could get some money so I can get a computer for Christmas or my birthday, which came first. I just talked about how I was in the Computer Club, but I didn't get to say much before she asked if I have a girl friend. She looked and talked in a rush and kept looking toward the bedroom. I asked her if she can stop being sick and live with us, and she said very soon, she promised, and that we're going to be together again.

My aunt Luisa came out, and Mami asked her in Spanish how she was doing. Luisa just said it was time that the visit ended. My mother started to beg her please to help her this one last time, and Luisa just opened the door. My mother started to curse her in Spanish, screaming loud curses, but Luisa just looked away holding the door open. She told me to go into the bedroom and close the door, but I couldn't move. Mami started punching the door, screaming at Luisa, calling her curse words in Spanish. Luisa said she would call the police. Mami looked at me with her face like in my dream. I ran into the bedroom and closed the door. A little later I heard the apartment door slam.

On Monday morning the whole school was talking about what had happened to Martin. He got into a knife fight with some guy. They found drugs on him, and he got busted. I guess he's in serious trouble. When my aunt heard it from the bodega man, she made me admit she was right about not letting me see him no more. Then came this lecture about how sometimes love is difficult, and you have to be strong to be good to people you love. Did I understand? I said yes. The next day I went to school thinking of a dream I had about how PR was so nice when my sister was there. We just sat on the balcony and drank the cold champagne cola my aunt Dalia would bring us in a glass with ice cubes. She always keeps her fridge stocked with champagne cola for us. Drinking it was especially nice after the afternoon bath, when my girl cousins always get dressed up and look so beautiful.

That's what I was thinking about when this kid next to me, Gregory, told me about Martin. Then the teachers really got on me all day. I had forgotten about my Friday history homework, and Brother Junius had told me to get a note from my aunt, and over the weekend I didn't make up that homework and forgot about the note. During homeroom Junius went to tell Sly, who said I couldn't go to Computer Club for a week. He said I had been messing around too much lately and sent me down to the principal's office. While I waited I thought of making some changes to my game. Maybe the wizard should be this big-time drug dealer, and he kidnaps your whole family and injects them with a drug that makes them invisible.

Bell was sent downstairs to the principal's office too. Brother Marcus had caught him showing that woman's picture around in the gym. But Bell was really an older guy and always looked like this kiddie school wasn't worth staying in anyway. He told me he didn't care what they did. I told him it was too bad they had caught him because I really wanted to see that woman again. He got up and looked around to see if some teacher was coming through the halls. Then he asked me if I had a dollar. I said no. I was lying. But he must have felt sorry for me because then he said to forget the buck. He pulled out his wallet and slipped out another shot. It was better than the first one with her smiling face behind her tits. Then Bell started whispering to me "Cruz Cruz" to warn me. Everybody calls me Cruz because my two last names in Spanish are Bonjour Cruz, and they get confused. I had the picture in my hand when the assistant principal came out of his office.

Bell got kicked out of school. That night when Luisa got home from work she wrote a note to the principal apologizing for me. She really chewed me out. I'm getting big enough to show some responsibility. If I don't pee in my bed no more I should be able to do what I'm supposed to so she can carry on with her life. Didn't I feel shame? I was always the best student in the class. Luckily the guy with the red Buick started honking downstairs. The next day with Luisa's note and my homework in shape, Brother Sly gave me a break and let me back into the Computer Club two days early. I told him about my idea of a wizard drug dealer, and he said no way.

Dalia called from PR because my sister had called her. She's living in Mayaguez with this man, and she's pregnant. She didn't want to come back. Dalia wants us to move back to PR with her because she's alone. Luisa asked me if I would want to return to PR and go to school there because maybe it's better for me. She was getting dressed and ready for something. You like it there better anyway, she said. I guessed maybe. What about her? She started to tell me something about being serious with this guy. While she put on her lipstick she told me she wanted me to meet him. Angelo's a really good guy that I would like. I asked her if I stayed would he be like my father. She looked at me surprised and said no, Angelo isn't a man who runs away from things. He's a real man. I meant if they were going to get like married and I lived with them, but when I tried to explain, Angelo started honking downstairs. She said she had to run, but that she would sit with me and talk to me later.

I was alone watching TV when somebody knocked on the door. I was afraid and looked through the peephole. I saw two policemen. I ran to the window to see if a real patrol car was parked in front of the building. It was. The policeman banged harder. I needed to go to the bathroom. He called me son and said it was the police. I put the chain on the door and opened it. He asked to see whatever grown up was there. I told him I live with my aunt and that I was alone. He gave me a piece of paper with a telephone number that my aunt should call. I was sleepy when my aunt came home, and I forgot about the paper. The next morning before she left for work I told her about the police.

Bell was allowed back into St. B's. His father talked to the principal, and everything was straightened out. The kids were saying the pictures really belonged to his old man, and Bell was bullshitting us with his sex stories. I didn't feel good in class and asked to go to the bathroom. I walked down the corridor and saw an empty classroom. The door was not locked, so I walked in. Walking into that empty room, I remembered about how in my adventure game the player searches through different rooms. I could hear the teacher in the class next door. His chalk squeaked against the blackboard. He could have been in this room, invisible like the kidnapped people in my game. The wizard drug dealer could have injected him with something to make him invisible.

I don't know how long I was sitting in that empty room, but Brother Marcus was going nuts. He came in and asked me if I was all right. They had been looking for me throughout the building. I had to go home right away. My aunt had called. I asked him if she was okay. He said he didn't know, but it was important that the principal Father Thompson take me home. Brother Marcus put his arm around my shoulder as we walked out the door and down the corridor. The classes were starting to come out for lunch, and the kids stared as they ran around us. In his office Father Thompson tried to explain to me that God had a strange way of doing things. That no matter what happens or how bad things get, I should never forget that God loves me. Did I understand? I said I did. His bald head shone brighter than ever. He continued to talk, and I thought of my game. The toughest part is making sure you still have some ransom left over so you don't remain a prisoner. If you can't ransom yourself, the game ends, and nobody you have saved can help you. I always knew that, but I just realized that the evil wizard drug dealer will keep you invisible forever.

Father Thompson put his arm around my shoulders as we walked down the block to my building. Angelo's red Buick was parked in front. Upstairs my aunt opened the door. Her eyes were red, and she hugged me very tightly. When she stopped hugging she took a step back and looked up at Father Thompson. He told her he had already spoken to me. She thanked him. She introduced me to Angelo, a big Italian guy with red cheeks and shining wet-looking hair. He was like a big strong nice guy with like a little guy's voice. After meeting me, he didn't say anything else, and I went to the window because just as we were coming to the building door, I thought I saw Martin, who they must have let out of jail. He was coming down the block with a girl that looked like Leticia.

Martin and the girl weren't anywhere, but I waited to see if they showed up as Luisa talked in a low voice so maybe I won't hear. She explained that her sister was completely different when she married my father. That was back in PR. Then he left her for another woman when I was still very little, and my mother got depressed. Luisa invited her to come to New York and start a new life. Unfortunately, Luisa said, she met this other man . . . and then she started crying. Father Thompson or Angelo must have calmed her down, because she spoke again and louder to tell Father that she had arranged for a cremation. He said that he would offer his morning mass for her the day after tomorrow. I heard them say all these things behind me. I was still looking out the window, but now I was thinking about the afternoon shower in Puerto Rico. If I was there I would be taking a shower and later doing my homework on the porch. I wished very much I could be there with my sister and my mom.

I was thinking this as Martin came out of Leticia's building. He wasn't wearing his gold chains. He looked up and waved at me. I waved back. I looked at Leticia's window. The shade was down. It had been down for days, and I hadn't seen her in a long time. I thought she had moved. Behind me my aunt was apologizing to Angelo because he would be late for work. He said he would take the day off and help her. She called me, and I turned around. They were all sitting drinking coffee. Then Father Thompson had to leave. He stood holding out his hand to me. He said he would arrange with Brother Sylvester about making up my semester exams.

I didn't go to school the next day, and Luisa didn't go to work. She cried and I just looked out the window a lot. She kept asking me if I was all right. The next morning we went to Father Thompson's seven o'clock mass. Some old Irish ladies were already in the church. Brother Sly came with Marcus Dimas and Junius. Even Mr. Tomasino, the gym teacher. They all came over to me and Luisa. She spoke to them. I looked at the pictures of heaven all around the church. Maybe my mother was there. Maybe I'll see her again, and her hands will be thin like they used to be when I was little.

When it was time for the sermon Father Thompson talked about our loved and departed ones whose souls are now with God. My aunt stroked the back of my head. I started thinking about Bell's picture of that woman. I never imagined a woman's hole like that. The woman gave a big white smile as she held her cunt open with her fingers. I wondered if it was a sin that I was thinking about that picture during mass. My aunt took my arm, and we stood up to go to the altar and receive communion. I looked back. Brother Marcus and Brother Sly and Mr. Tomasino stood in line behind us. Then the little old ladies. After mass we went to see Father Thompson in the rectory. He asked me how I was feeling. He and my aunt talked about the problem and what would be best for me. He said the counselor told him I should snap out of it. They looked at me, and I smiled at them.

That was three months ago. I didn't have my computer then. Angelo got me this PC for their wedding present, a PC better than the ones in school, with a color monitor and the WordStar word processor with spelling checker. It also has a drawing program and some video games. I'm trying to finish my adventure game, but without Brother Sly I've got to figure out a lot on my own. I printed out the program and wrote him a letter asking him to help me. I gave the letter and the program to Luisa to mail for me. She told the doctor about the letter and the program and that I spend my time writing on the computer. He gives me these kind of puzzles to do then asks me questions but says it's okay if I don't answer. What kind of game am I writing? Is the evil wizard like anybody I knew? What is it that I am writing? Is it a story or a diary? He tells me that one day soon I should be ready to talk and not just write on my PC.

The Duck

Marco popped into the kitchen just as his mother said something in Spanish about a duck at his sister Tina's birthday party. Aunt Norma was mixing a dip for chips while Mami arranged poultry pieces in a baking pan. Marco asked if what she prepared was duck, because he had never eaten duck and didn't know if he would like it.

"No," she explained in English, "this is chicken."

"So what did you say before about a duck at the party?"

Mami gave a confused look at Norma, then giggled.

"Oh, . . . well, a duck in Spanish is a man who moves his behind from side to side, like a duck, when he walks."

"Like Carla?" The next-door neighbor, famous in the building for her sway in tight pants.

Mami smiled at Norma again, "Yes."

"Then when is this duck going to get here?"

Mami looked at Norma again before answering. She said that she had been only joking about somebody who said he might stop by. "But you should never call anybody a duck in Spanish because it isn't nice. Now run and tell Tina to get out of the bathtub."

Marco shouted Mami's instructions to Tina through the bathroom door, then stood in front of the body-length mirror, admiring his outfit: Western hat, boots, shirt—a plump, olive-skinned cowboy. He looked forward to showing Papi his cowboy outfit with a bandanna, like the brightly colored handkerchiefs Papi sometimes wears in the open collar of his shirts.

The door swung back and Tina tiptoed out, wrapped in a towel and still dripping wet, hollering that she was out. Fastidious Tina had refused to get ready until the very last second. The door buzzer sounded, and Marco ran to get the door, almost crashing into Mami on her way to dress up Tina.

He had hoped his Papi was at the door, but from the long continuous buzz he knew it was his six-year-old cousin, Little Eddie. Marco opened the door and yanked Eddie's hand from the buzzer. Eddie hugged Marco and began to tickle him. He always did that. Aunt Norma came out of the kitchen, and Eddie stopped tickling to give her a kiss on the cheek. She asked why he was alone. He explained that his father had walked with him up the stairs but then remembered that he didn't pick up the ice cream he was asked to bring. "Whatcha doin,' gordo?"

"Why do you say I'm gordo?"

"Cause you're the chubbiest kid I know."

"Where's Freddy? Isn't he coming?"

"Yeah, he went with my dad. Let's watch television."

"No, there's going to be a party, stupid."

"Yeah, where? I don't see hats or nothing."

"Mami has them hidden, so creeps like you don't stomp on them." They walked into the living room as Tina came out of the bedroom wearing a white dress and her long black hair in two pony tails. Mami's outstretched hands pointed toward precious Tina as if introducing an act. "Well? Aren't you two *caballeros* going to tell her how nice she looks? That's what men do when a lady gets dressed up."

"She's my sister."

"So what? She's a girl."

"So what if I don't like girls?"

Mami's eyes let Marco know he shouldn't have said that. Reading into his mother's look a violent reaction, he was ready to raise his arms in defense. But Mami simply shook her head as she grabbed Tina's hand and led her to the kitchen.

"My brother Freddy once said that, and my dad gave him a mean slap." The door buzzed twice. Marco started for the door, but Eddie stopped him: "That's just my dad. He always buzzes twice." Eddie ran to the door, and Marco sat on the sofa. He remembered when he started imitating the way Carla walks his Mami got furious because "Boys don't go around acting like girls."

Uncle Ed and cousin Freddy arrived, and Marco listened to the salutations and kisses and Ed's "Oh how nice Tina looks!" Little Eddie jumped up and down, wanting to know what flavor ice cream they had gotten. Ed told him vanilla and chocolate and to calm down. Tina and Little Eddie went to the living room, but Marco lingered in the foyer beside the kitchen, hoping maybe his Papi would ring the buzzer. He heard Norma thank Ed for the ice cream. She was always nice to Ed and always poking fun at him. *"Well, are you behaving?"* she asked him in Spanish. *"Have you ever seen me misbehave, Norma?" "No, I haven't had that pleasure." "Well, that can be arranged." "Why don't you bring your sweet wife, so she can hear you?" "I left her at her mother's. You know how she feels about my side of the family, or maybe it's just you she doesn't like, Norma." "This man is shameless, but what else can I expect from a Bonjour?" "But Norma, at least one of the Bonjours is very different, isn't that true, Eduardo?" "Oh sure, nena, different only in the direction he takes to get lost. Otherwise he's just like all of them, guided by the same antenna."*

Uncle Ed said, "I better see how the kids are doing," and surprised to see Marco standing by the door. "Hey, partner! How're you doing?" He squeezed Marco's shoulders, and they both stepped into the living room. "Let's visit the kids, see what they're doing. Hey, did your Papi call?

"Yeah, he wished Tina a happy birthday this morning."

"What'd he say about coming?"

"He's coming after work."

"Well, good, that's, . . . that's good," he said, looking around the walls as if he seriously planned to paint the living room. "Well, so what were you guys up to—hey, Freddy, tell Marco about your new video game."

"Yeah, I finally got it."

"Is it the one with the karate man and the girl, just like in the video game room?"

"Yeah, it's awesome, man. You hear the punches and the kicks, and the bad guys yell things at him, and the girl crying out for help. But guess what? My joystick is broke. And guess who broke it?" His head bounced stiff-necked in the direction of Little Eddie and Uncle Eddie.

"The shrimp."

"No, booger nose, wrong again."

Freddy pointed to his father. "Monster Lobster over here with his he-man claws."

"Okay, smart guy, who has the highest score?"

Little Eddie jumped in: "I do."

"That's right, I forgot. I mean between Freddy and me. Boy, you ungrateful runts. After all the hours I've put in playing with you. Not all fathers do that." His head jerked back and he looked around at the walls again.

Little Eddie wanted to play a video game.

"We're having a party. See?"

Mami had just come into the room and placed a pair of full shopping bags on the sofa. From one bag she took out a stack of pointed party hats and handed one each to her nephews, who immediately put them on. Then she took out a batch of red cardboard letters and asked Freddy and Uncle Ed to help her. First, Uncle Ed's long arms spread out a large, festooned HAPPY BIRTHDAY, which Mami taped to the wall behind the sofa. Freddy and Uncle Ed then taped small metallic Happy Birthday signs around the room. Marco and Little Eddie were ordered to each get a dining table chair that Freddy was assigned to position in diagonally opposite corners. Standing on one chair, Mami handed Marco the pink crepe paper to unroll until it extended to Uncle Ed on the other chair. Then the chairs were switched to the other corners, and Marco unrolled another pink strip that crossed the first one. When Uncle Ed taped the intersecting streams to the lighting fixture, a giant pink X sagged from the ceiling. Standing directly under the X's center, Marco had the sensation of standing in the eye of the room's crystallizing magic, and then, to complete his fantasy, from the other shopping bag Mami pulled up by her finger a wire loop attached to a piñata in the form of a rooster.

The Duck

It was red, its fat body covered with feathers of bright red tissue paper and its head crowned with a darker-red ribbon paper crest. Uncle Ed held it up and looked at it. "This a real macho rooster with long claws for fighting," he said as he raised it by the wire loop and tied it to the end of the long cord that he had wrapped around the lighting fixture. Then, by making a big loopy knot, he shortened the chord until it was time to lower the rooster and break it open. Tina complained that Little Eddie was laughing at her because she called it a chicken. Mami scolded Little Eddie for being cruel and explained to Tina that a rooster is a boy chicken, so it couldn't lay eggs and have chicks. But Mami quickly reminded the children that even though a rooster can't lay eggs, this rooster was full of candy. So, Marco summarized to himself, this piñata rooster is a like a boy chicken that lays candy instead of eggs. Whatever it was, it sure was the giant switch that truly juiced the party. Tina bounced clapping as she thanked Mami for such a divine touch.

The buzzer began announcing the arrival of Tina's friends, with their gifts and their parents. Marco opened the door every time. Aunt Norma made certain that every kid received a party hat.

When all the kids had arrived, Ed became the ringmaster and ordered the bigger boys to bring in all the dining table chairs for a round of musical chairs only for the littlest kids. As Freddy played a cassette of *merengue* music, the smaller ones walked fast around the chairs until he turned off the music. Ed sternly disqualified the boys who bumped off the girls. Three rounds of play were needed to get boy and girl winners. A girl named Linda was given a little white stuffed poodle, and Little Eddie received a rolled up kite, which he wanted to spread open right there until his father grabbed it and took it into Mami's bedroom for safekeeping.

After that, as the stereo played salsa, Uncle Ed started a dance contest, holding up two dollars to be given to the best couple. The kids all danced furiously in pairs, boy and girl. At the end of the record, a little boy named Elvis and a girl named Maria were awarded the money. Ed then invited the watching parents to dance, and as they danced, the boys and a few girls took turns at the TV video game while most of the girls dressed and undressed Tina's collection of dolls.

The cutting of the cake was supposed to follow the dance contest, according to what Tina was told by Mami, who instead started serving the children dinner on plastic plates as Norma and the other mothers served the parents. Marco ate, listening for the door buzzer, hoping that his Papi would arrive before the cutting of the cake, which Mami now said would take place after dinner.

But after the plastic plates made the round trip back to the kitchen, Mami announced to the children that Tina was going to open her presents. Tina sat on the sofa with the presents piled at her feet and started opening the packages. Most were clothes, but she also received a Parcheesi game and Chinese checkers and new clothes for her Barbie doll. When done with the presents, Tina asked if next she would be cutting the cake, but Mami answered, "It's still early so we can wait while I clean up." Mami and Aunt Norma disappeared to the kitchen, where, after a little while, Marco went to inquire about the cake and also when his father would come. Just then the buzzer sounded.

Marco ran to door and, on opening it, his day-long anticipation gushed out: "Papi!" He hugged his Papi's waist. Tina threw herself at her father's knees, hugging tightly. Papi put down a stuffed shopping bag and squatted to hug them back, "My princess and my cowboy. You both look great!" Papi looked okay in the gray suit but strange compared to the other fathers in guayaberas and short-sleeved shirts. Aunt Norma came to the door to welcome him.

He lifted Tina, carried her on his forearm. His other arm fell over Marco's shoulders. Marco felt good with his head on his Papi's ribs, in his cloud of cologne. And there was the shopping bag that Marco volunteered to carry. Papi entered the living room tossing out a big *"Hola!"*

Tina asked about the presents in the bag.

"Okay, boss lady. You know you're my boss lady." He put Tina down and removed his jacket, which he draped over the back of the sofa. "Here, this one is for you. Happy Birthday." He kissed Tina's cheek as she admired the largest wrapped package.

Surrounded by kids, Tina tore away the wrapping. A large Wonder Woman doll half her size posed in a cellophane window. Tina pulled it out of the box, calling Mami to come and see it. Little Eddie ran into the kitchen with the message, and Mami came in drying her hands with her apron. She greeted Papi cordially and turned her attention to Tina, who was showing around her doll. Meanwhile Papi took out the long, flat package that, back at the door, Marco had guessed was for him. Papi always brought something for each of them. "Here you are, pardner." Marco took his gift and looked in the bag, which appeared to contain something else, but the only thing left in it was a newspaper.

What Marco found under the wrapping was perfect: in a box decorated with jungle foliage dotted with doomed yellow-skinned men was a battery-powered replica of Rambo's automatic rifle. Marco gave his Papi a big kiss, pulled his new acquisition out of its Styrofoam mold, pulled back on a lever, and started aiming the rifle's automatic hacking at Little Eddie. The rifle passed hands from Freddy to Little Eddie to the three other boys at the party as the music played and parents talked or danced, but Marco stayed by his Papi, who told Uncle Ed about a nice white shirt saved for him, a gift from one of the stores where he works. Papi designed store windows for men's stores. Marco once heard Uncle Ed say that he prayed that Papi's talent wasn't hereditary.

Little Eddie, having lost control of the rifle to his older brother, stormed off: "Keep it! I heard Rambo is really a faggot."

"Oh yeah, right," Marco poked his elbow into Freddy's ribs.

"Shut up, fatso, 'cause nobody's talking to you."

"Hey, you two. Stop this right now." Uncle Ed was furious.

"Isn't it true, Papi, didn't your friend say in Spanish that Rambo was really a duck, and that's a faggot, right?"

"Eddie, I said drop it." Uncle's pointing finger was a muzzle aimed between Little Eddie's eyes.

Just then Aunt Norma came into the living room carrying a foldable domino table that she opened directly across from the sofa. Mami unfurled a paper spread with a big Snoopy in the center. Snoopy paper plates, cups, and napkins were then piled in a neat row along one side of the table. Finally Aunt Norma, bearing the lighted cake, started the parents into the room, a chorus singing

"Happy Birthday." As Norma positioned the cake on top of Snoopy, Tina ran over to stand beside Mami. The pointy-hatted children surrounded the cake, singing along, their eyes a wide circle of shining beads like those on the frosting. The grownups stood behind the children, Papi joining the circle. Tina was so happy that she forgot about the missing front tooth she didn't want everybody to see. When the singing of "Happy Birthday" ended, Tina made a wish and blew out the candles in a sudden bright flash. Aunt Norma had taken a picture.

Tina wanted a special shot. "I want you to take one with me and Papi, holding the knife, like we're cutting the cake together." Marco remembered that the pose was identical to the large picture in Mami's wedding album, her hand under Papi's, both hands wrapped around the handle. Flash.

"Now with the big guy. Come on, my main man." Tina, Papi, and Marco cut the cake. Flash.

The kids were getting restless, but there were a two more pictures to take, Mami with Tina, then Mami, Tina, and Marco.

Mami finally started cutting the cake. She passed the pieces on plastic plates to Papi, who added a side clump of ice cream and doled out the dishes to the waiting line of children. Aunt Norma served the parents. Everybody ate cake except Freddy, who took the opportunity to play a video game.

The phone rang. Marco answered. The call was for Papi. Some man. Mami lowered the stereo and ordered the children to hush so Papi could hear the voice on the phone. For a few seconds the only sounds were of Freddy's clicking the joystick, the video karate guy's yells, and the squish every time Mami stuffed frosting-smeared plastic plates into a garbage bag. She was crushing the plates hard, as if she were angry at them. Marco was already familiar with that mood, the one that came over her when he used to ask her why Papi couldn't live with them.

With his back turned to the party, Papi looked at his watch and explained that he wasn't sure what time. Around the room, the faces of the grownups were holding in a laugh, as if somebody had told a joke.

While Papi was still talking, Mami raised the volume of the music before carrying off a bulging plastic bag back to the kitchen. Some of the parents found that funny; Marco lowered the volume again. When Papi hung up, Aunt Norma served him a plate with cake and ice cream and reminded him of the party's remaining event, pointing to the ceiling. Papi looked up and nodded. Uncle Ed asked one of the parents to let him borrow a chair. Standing on it, he untied the cord and the fat red rooster hung into the middle of the living room.

Papi asked the kids if they knew what that red rooster was. Most of the kids knew and yelled it out. "Right. That's a piñata, and he's got a belly full of candies inside. But you have to break him open so the candies can fall out. Which one of you thinks you're strong enough to do that?"

He was mobbed by little raised hands and cries of "Me, me, me!"

"Okay, you'll all get a chance. Now we need something to break it with."

"A broomstick," Freddy suggested.

"Too dangerous."

"How about with our hands?" That was Little Eddie.

Marco had gone into his room and returned with a hollow plastic bat.

"That's my boy. This is perfect." He explained to the kids about being blindfolded and spun around before taking a swing. One try each. "Okay, now Tina first because she's the birthday girl. Let's use Marco's bandanna." Papi blindfolded Tina, spun her around once, but then positioned her directly under the piñata and held it in place. Tina hit the rooster squarely without ruffling its paper feathers. All five of the other little girls took their turns and each hit the piñata, held fixed for them, without noticeable effects. Confident no girl would smash it, the boys haggled over who should get the honor.

Marco, figuring that the one who bashed open the rooster would lose out because everybody else would grab the goodies, refused to take the bat. Little Eddie insisted on being first, so Papi let him try, but tipping the piñata so it swayed. Blindfolded and spun around, Little Eddie flailed away, hitting nothing, until he was stopped before he hurt somebody. Papi tried to convince Marco, who deferred to his bigger cousin. Freddy agreed because he really didn't want candies anyway. An anxious circle formed around Freddy.

He held the bat tightly, taking cautious half-steps. Little Eddie goaded him with "Come on, don't take any sissy swipes," and Marco echoed with, "Yeah, no sissy swipes." Papi pushed the piñata so it swirled and swayed in circles but Freddy seemed to have a radar fix on that fat paper rooster. His first swipe snipped off the tail, but no candies fell out. The gang applauded, and Freddy removed his blindfold to see what he had accomplished.

Excited by the promise of candies, the kids all urged that Freddy try again. Papi intervened: one shot apiece. He tried to convince Marco to make the decisive strike: "Now Marco can break it, what d'you say?" But the kids weren't buying, including Marco, who wanted to be ready to grab as many candies as he could. No, Freddy was everybody's man. "Fred-dy! Fred-dy! Fred-dy!" So Papi blindfolded him again, spun him several times, and tipped the piñata so it would swing.

As if he had eyes pasted on his blindfold, however, Freddy reared back, and suddenly the rooster's belly burst with a thunderclap under whose rainfall children dove to grab at cellophane-wrapped hard candy. The excitement seemed to exhaust just about everybody, as the adults all gave signs of having had enough. The fathers stood one by one, each lifting their pants by the belt and taking a deep breath, a gesture that always signified "It's getting late." At Marco's birthday party the parents stayed to dance until late, but today was Sunday. Papi didn't make it to that party because he had the flu.

At least Papi stayed behind, although he was already wearing his suit jacket. Marco and Tina begged him to take it off and stay, and he sat on the sofa and lifted Tina onto his lap. He explained that he had been working all day and needed to go home and rest. He promised to pick them up next weekend and take them somewhere special. Where? He didn't know yet. He kissed them both and gave them a long, firm hug. He had made such promises before but not kept them.

When he reached the foyer, Aunt Norma saw him at the door. Before leaving, he poked his head into the dining room to say good-bye to Mami in the kitchen. She was scrubbing the sink and looked up, said good night, then went back to cleaning. Aunt Norma was holding the door open. Papi kissed and hugged Tina and Marco one final time. Marco begged him to keep his word about next week.

That night Marco couldn't sleep, wondering to what special place Papi would take them. In the night's silence he heard his Mami and Aunt Norma talking in Spanish in the dining room. *Did you read this about another Bonjour? Hear, look. I don't think this Bonjour is related to ours. I never heard of him. Have you? No? Apparently he came from a better branch than what I married. Look where he lived. But then it says here that he fell into this drug situation because of a woman gang member. That sounds more like a Bonjour. Oh, by the way, it was a really nice and delicious cake that Doña Lydia made. . . .*

Hearing his Mami and Aunt Norma talk about the birthday cake made him hungry. He climbed down from his upper bunk bed and tiptoed past the snoring Tina. As he approached the dining room, he paused, unsure if Mami would be glad to see him out of bed so late. He waited to decide, but his craving got worse . . . *Yes, but look what happened to me. I get the only duck. You know where that came from, the mother's side where except for her they all came out that way. Ay, did you hear that phone conversation after we cut the cake?*

He had forgotten about the duck. Eddie had said that a duck in Spanish is a faggot and that Rambo was a duck. Marco envisioned a Rambo-looking guy, who moved his behind when he walked and was a faggot, which everybody knows is somebody who is chicken. He'd heard the word a million times at school. "You can't climb that fence? Why, you a faggot?" "You wouldn't hit him back? Why, you a faggot?" But now his only real interest sat in the cake box on the table. He walked into the kitchen wearing a sad face.

Mami held out her arms to receive him. After she stroked his hair a few times, he asked if he could have a piece of cake.

"Well, if you eat your piece now, the rest belongs to Tina."

He understood.

But instead of getting up to cut the cake, she just looked at him.
"Mami, come oooon. I'm hungry."
"You promise not to complain later when Tina has her piece?"
"OK. I promise."
"You promise you're not trying to fool me?"
"No, I'm not fooling you."

Mami held his face in her hands and looked long into his eyes until he slipped from her tender hold because Aunt Norma had placed a dish and was about to open the cake box to cut a piece. Marco stared at the ruins of that once beautiful cake. Seeing how little was left, he was glad that duck never did show up.

The Flowering of Isabel

Elizabeth Bonjour had just entered the crowded subway car and squeezed into a space facing the seated passengers when the one in front of her, a man in a blue pinstripe suit, got up and offered his seat. Her first impulse was to decline, but as he was already standing, and she was so tired after her evening marketing class that she simply thanked him and occupied the seat.

Once seated, she sensed that the man, attractive with wavy black hair and who could have been Latin himself or as well Middle Eastern, was silently addressing her, not rudely or brazenly but in a subtler, flattering way. But she wasn't about to pick up a man in a subway, and she had to study. She removed the textbook from her briefcase and read until she noticed that the book's top edge cut across the man's pinstriped crotch. She put the book flat on her lap. At the next stop, the man turned, and his crown of wavy black hair floated out among the exiting passengers.

His looks reminded her of her classmate Luis, who had started to arrive early to class and sit next to her. That very night he had invited her to have dinner with him after class, and she turned him down. She couldn't believe how much that exiting man resembled Luis. Even more important, she couldn't believe she was tempted to accept Luis's invitation.

For the past six years, her life had been simplified by routine. Weekday mornings she boarded a subway in Brooklyn to Manhattan, where she cared for Mrs. Farber's baby Jimmy. For the first half of the day, she studied as he slept. In the afternoon, she took Jimmy out in his stroller along Madison Avenue. Three nights a week she attended night classes at Hunter College, conveniently just blocks away from Mrs. Farber's. Then she rode the subway back to Brooklyn. On Fridays she went straight home to relax and devote the weekend to catching up on schoolwork. Graduating had been her unwavering, central ambition, and now, in her final spring semester, she had become curious about the worldly things she had kept at bay, dating being one of them.

She had, of course, dated before, a couple of boyfriends in high school and when she worked as an office temp, but she never really felt they were a serious step toward a future in which she saw herself. Once, she was actually engaged, the breakup sowing her determination to study. Only now, on the verge of graduating, did she allow herself to seriously contemplate that future with herself reinvented, no longer the uncertain young daughter of a woman who cleaned offices at night but someone on her way to becoming a grown, confident woman like those she observed along Madison Avenue, dressed in the fine clothes that she fleetingly admired in store windows without pausing to torture herself with desires beyond her means.

That very afternoon, in fact, as she pushed Jimmy in his stroller, she paused briefly to look at a beltless silk dress with a Chinese collar, a soft turquoise with little green swirling leaves, and helplessly imagined wearing it, her normally pony-tailed black hair loose and flowing. That fantasy lasted only a second before she saw her reflection in the storefront glass: a plain-looking young woman in a trench coat, clutching Jimmy's stroller. As she walked away, she imagined the embarrassment of pricing the dress then looking ridiculous as she took off her coat while still in her white working uniform.

She made the mistake of telling her mother about the dress, and her mother warned her yet again about the danger of forgetting her real life for fantasy after their meeting with that lawyer. He had informed Isabel that her father's widow had established a trust fund with "substantial money" that would be enough to give her security but whose exact amount could not be revealed until she reached the age of thirty, when she would receive the money.

The lawyer and papers may have said whatever they said, but for her mother there was no guarantee that Isabel would inherit anything. Now that she's an old lonely woman, Javier's wife Martina may be feeling bad that she made her husband promise never to see his child, but so much could happen. Martina has two grandsons, also her blood, and what if they took legal action to get that money? And why didn't she just give the money outright, now that her son was dead and she didn't need it all to live out her simple life in Puerto Rico? This legal arrangement could just be a way of easing her conscience temporarily until she felt better, thought it over, and then took the money back. Supposedly this trust was set up to protect Isabel from immaturity, from a youthful inability to see through a handsome but treacherous young suitor who might both break her heart and spend all the money. This very noble explanation for a bunch of papers that don't reimburse Isabel for the pain . . . her mother went on and on like that.

Isabel listened patiently, sympathizing with her mother's resentment that for all those years Martina's anger was misplaced on her, also a victim of Javier's deceptions, as over the years she would swear to her relatives, who had warned her of the Bonjours. For at first her mother didn't know that Javier was married. He said that he found her irresistible, a pretty widow living with her young divorced niece and her baby, a compact family that offered a loving place, and so he visited frequently, patiently courting. He carried on the deception for months until her mother told him that she was pregnant, after which he stayed away for weeks.

Her mother once obliquely admitted in tears that maybe the conception was no accident, that she had long wanted a child, and at another time she let slip that before she had conceived she did know that he was still married. But she also claimed that Javier had sworn that he was in the process of leaving Martina and moving out. That was the only reason why she had allowed Javier to come into their lives, she insisted, because she had her principles and wasn't a husband stealer. Now Martina's sudden intrusion in their lives had reopened painful wounds, and a part of her wished that her daughter could decline this inheritance. But that would only do Isabel harm.

Whoever was the conduit, she also reasoned, Lizzy was entitled to this palpable presence of her father. "But only if you learn the lesson that both Martina and I are teaching you about Latin men, because if the Bonjours may be the worst example, they are not much worse than the ones we think are good," she said to Isabel, who understood that her mother also tacitly referred to her first, real husband, who had died in the Vietnam War, about whom she never once said an ill word—although neither did she ever say a joyful one.

Isabel had listened respectfully and even sympathetically to her mother's outburst on expensive fantasies but hadn't forgotten about the dress, or rather the vague something that it represented for her. Maybe its being in that forbidden boutique is what challenged her, enticed her, and while waiting for her mother to serve a warmed-up dinner, Isabel decided that on the weekend she would walk through the store like someone who belonged in it and try on that dress. On Saturday, she rode the subway to Manhattan but this time looking business-like, in a skirt and blouse and a tweed sport jacket. The saleslady treated her courteously, and she seemed to hold up well, although she felt extremely self-conscious of feigning at being comfortable. The dress, she was told, was discounted to four hundred and seventy-five dollars. Would she like to try it on?

She never imagined the price would be that high, and although she wanted to try it on and see herself in it, she lost her nerve. She thanked the saleswoman and went home. On Monday, when she and Jimmy passed the store, the dress was no longer in the window. She stood holding on to the stroller and looking up and down Madison Avenue. The dress's absence had emptied her stroll of a purpose more interesting than taking Jimmy out for fresh air. And being so close to never having to take this stroll again, she no longer wanted to pass the same stores as a nanny dressed in her white uniform even if under her coat. Standing undecided on a corner of Madison, her gaze followed the traffic north. Up there, beyond *this* Madison Avenue, Luis explained to her, everything changed and became El Barrio. Luis still lived there with his family while he finished his studies. She had never been to El Barrio. She was born and grew up in Brooklyn and didn't know anybody up there.

A bus stopped in front of her, discharged and took on passengers, and she watched it shrink as it rode uptown toward Luis's El Barrio. She looked at Jimmy, who had fallen asleep. What could happen if she boarded the next bus with him? People certainly didn't eat children up there. Her mother, if she knew her daughter had this notion in her head, would give her a long sermon. She took Jimmy home.

The following afternoon they had just started their stroll, and she happened to stop to adjust Jimmy in the stroller and realized that she was standing by a bus stop. A northbound bus was also a block away and approaching. She made a sudden decision. Jimmy, cute in his blue jumpsuit with a big yellow bird on his chest, probably wondered why he was being removed from the stroller. "This is the first time you're going to El Barrio too, isn't it?" Jimmy giggled back. The bus came and she boarded it, cradling Jimmy in one arm, with the folded stroller's dual hook handles hanging from the other arm.

The passengers were mostly gray-haired seniors. The driver waited for her to reach the back, where she sat with Jimmy on her lap. The bus climbed numbered streets, past storefronts, galleries, banks, building entrances. After crossing 96th Street, the tonality of everything changed. Buildings became dingier, the pedestrians and bus passengers were now darker complexioned.

She got off at 116th Street, which she knew was El Barrio because Luis said he lived on 118th but way east by Third Avenue. A young man in a bomber jacket helped her carry the stroller off the bus. Looking around at the almost deserted sidewalk, she was suddenly unnerved. The street was surrounded by old and run-down-looking residential buildings with bodegas and small stores on the sidewalk. So this was El Barrio, and now that she had dared to discover it, there seemed to be nothing more to do than push Jimmy briskly toward Lexington Avenue, where she could take the southbound bus. When she reached the corner of Park Avenue—not the Park Avenue with well-tended, flower-decorated dividers, but a darker avenue under the elevated tracks of the suburban train lines that were subterranean further south—she saw a sign that announced La Marketa. Luis had mentioned this supposedly famous market in barracks-like enclosures under the elevated tracks. He couldn't believe that people from Brooklyn, even Ricans, are so different: "You're Puerto Rican, and you never heard of La Marketa?"

Mainly women were walking in and out of the market, some with strollers like her, so she followed one of them, who held the door open, and suddenly she was engulfed in the competing smells and sights of shining piles of fruits and vegetables, displays of fresh silvery fish and red meats, pyramids of canned groceries. She unbuttoned her coat. While she looked around, a robust fruit man gave Jimmy a grape. She immediately grabbed it.

"It's okay, lady. They're seedless." He had an Italian accent.

She split open the grape and returned its halves to Jimmy, then thanked the man.

"Your baby is pretty like you."

She smiled at him and walked on, pondering the fruit man's compliment. Downtown no one mistook her for Jimmy's mother. Was it because of her complexion, which wasn't much darker than Mrs. Farber's, herself a brunette? Jimmy was as yet nondescript, and her coat normally covered over her white uniform. Were the white stockings the clue? Or was it something subtler?

Engrossed in this thought she stepped into a cloud of fragrance. It floated toward her from a cluttered counter of different-sized candles, jars filled with herbs, religiously labeled aerosol cans, religious pictures, strands of beads and a glass display of statues, wood and leather crafts, records and cassettes. She had never been to a *botánica,* which is what the sign over the counter said: Botánica Madrazo.

"*Tengo algo que le va a gustar.* I have something that you're going to like," a black woman said as she came out from behind the counter. She also wore all white, a white dress and white stockings. "It's something perfect for a woman as devout as you. Wait." She stooped behind a display counter and came up with a leather folder. She brought it around to the front of the counter. "This is a genuine leather cover." She pointed to the pouch of Jimmy's stroller, to the notebook that Elizabeth always carried so she could study on a park bench when Jimmy dozed off. "That notebook fits in this cover. Look." The woman opened the cover and over the front inside flap was embossed the image of what Elizabeth thought was the Virgin

Mary standing on a snake that writhed over the sickle edge of a half-moon. "Santa Barbara will be with you everywhere, protect you as you, a lady of faith, already know." The woman looked for something around Elizabeth's neck, maybe the stream of bead necklaces flowing down and under her own white dress.

Elizabeth pulled up her coat collar, politely declined, and she started to walk on, but the woman asked her to please wait, because she really felt that Santa Barbara wanted her to have this cover. She asked permission to handle the notebook, then fitted the cover and handed it back. It was indeed a fine-looking cover, and the woman reduced the price by five dollars. Elizabeth thanked her but declined again, so the woman reduced it by another five dollars. It was now only ten dollars, half its price and real leather, the woman pointed out. She felt very strongly that Santa Barbara would be pleased.

It was after all a nice cover, and having Santa Barbara's image inside really didn't bother her. As the lady wrote out a sales slip, Elizabeth browsed over more of the merchandise: aerosol cans of mists to inspire love, purify the air of loneliness or make you fertile, large bottles of leaves and herbs, rows of framed pictures of saints and angels, variously sized painted plaster statues of Jesus and Santa Barbara, and an assortment of statues of Indians in full-feathered head dress, from busts to standing figures. Everything seemed exotic and spooky. Her eyes met those of the woman, who had been observing her.

"That baby is not yours, I know. But you are a special person who will find everything you truly desire in life. Santa Barbara is watching over you. Please, give me your hand." Apprehensive, Isabel extended her hand. The woman anointed its back with a warm oil. "I will pray for you and your own baby." She handed Isabel a calling card: *Señora Madrazo*. "Please call me if you have problems. I give consultations." Elizabeth paid, and suddenly drained, having gotten as much of La Marketa as she could handle, she turned Jimmy in the direction of the exit.

Outside she quickly got her bearings and continued east on 116th Street, along a beehive of shops that offered dresses, records, toys that poured out on the sidewalk, a spectacle complete with a sound-track of amplified salsa. Elizabeth paused at a dress shop with several racks jutting out onto the sidewalk. What dresses, she thought, were only worth $10 and $15? She passed her hand across a rack whose selection was more appropriate for an older woman. Another rack offered more of the same.

Her hand was making an indifferent parting sweep through a third rack, but these dresses were really different, more like something she might want to wear. Luis, she remembered, had the women students flocking around him after he gave a talk in their economics class on markup value and how some communities form markdown economies, giving as illustration a place on 116th Street where one could get dresses, defective or out of season or gotten through ways one better not investigate, that originally cost hundreds more on the Upper East Side.

This rack had no sign with prices above it. She picked out two she might consider although not really her size and requiring that her cousin Carmen, who had recently moved to an apartment on the floor above hers, make alterations. She measured them on her before Jimmy, who giggled. She returned them to the rack while deciding whether to take them, and at that moment Jimmy became restless and started to cry. She crouched to put the pacifier dangling from his neck in his mouth and recline the stroller's back so he could sleep. As she tucked him in, her eye caught a glimpse of what she thought was a familiar green and blue.

She pushed aside dresses and there before her eyes hung the same turquoise, the same little leaves. She inspected the dress thoroughly. It was one size too large, with one seam torn half the length of the dress, things that Carmen could work on. The label had been cut off. When she asked for the price, the man explained that these dresses were more expensive. She pointed out the torn seam. Thirty dollars was his price, which she paid happily. Feeling redeemed and afraid she had spent more time uptown than she had planned, she took Jimmy straight to Lexington, where a woman ordered her young boy to help the mother lift the stroller into the bus.

When she got home that night, her mother and Carmen couldn't believe her good luck at finding this gorgeous dress at a clearance rack in Bloomingdales, in whose distinctive shopping bag—taken from Mrs. Farber's many in a kitchen closet—she brought it home. Elizabeth knew that her mother would have never understood why her daughter went to El Barrio and, worse yet, was crazy enough to take Jimmy with her. Looking back, she couldn't believe it herself and thanked God that nothing happened, as Mrs. Farber would have probably accused her of attempting to kidnap Jimmy. And, of course, how could she find the words to make any sense to her mother of being made curious about El Barrio by a classmate named Luis.

Carmen fixed the dress. Elizabeth came home from class to find it hanging beautifully. She gave her cousin a big hug then rushed to try it on. They both stood before the mirror speechless. How could she wait one month to wear it for graduation. Tomorrow night, she told Carmen, there was an awards ceremony and reception for graduating students. She hadn't thought of going, having not won any awards herself, but the entire class talked of being there, and now she couldn't resist.

Carmen, as close to her as a sister, was delighted to see her cousin beside herself with such rare enthusiasm for anything that might attract a mate. And so was their mother. "Well, finally. It's good to see you behaving like a normal woman."

That comment surprised Elizabeth because, if anyone, it was her mother who had caused her to be reluctant to behave "like a normal woman."

"Mami, I just happened to like the dress."

Later in her bedroom, as she put her hair in rollers, there was a knock at her door. Her mother didn't wait for an answer and opened. She paused to observe her daughter in rollers. "Now don't tell me you are going through all this trouble for nothing. So who is this magician?"

"Mami, there's no man." Elizabeth turned to finish curling her hair. "I just like the dress." Her mother would never understand that the dress also symbolized her new life, her *graduating* in so many senses that she couldn't put into words.

Her mother raised her eyebrows and smirked.

"I told you. There is a reception for graduating students tomorrow night."

Her mother chuckled. "You look gorgeous in that dress, *mi hija*. You are lying to yourself about the man and I hope that you finally realize it."

The following morning, sunny and with the promise of a much warmer afternoon, she wore the dress under an open spring coat. As she walked in appropriately matched shoes, a glow seeped out, catching the eyes of both men and women. Her radiance even slowed down Mrs. Farber, a woman always too rushed to notice anything. Holding a batch of papers that were about to go into her attaché case, she said, "That dress is quite fetching on you."

She explained about the reception that night, but as Mrs. Farber continued preparing her papers, she took side glances as if suspecting that Elizabeth's real intention was to show her up. Maybe she recognized the dress from the boutique window, Elizabeth thought. Maybe she's surprised that I should show such good taste. Maybe she's thinking that I'm getting paid way too much. Whatever thoughts produced that look, before Mrs. Farber left, Elizabeth made certain to be wearing her white uniform. That afternoon, before taking Jimmy outside, she changed into her dress.

When she crossed the lobby, this time carrying her coat, the doorman tipped his cap in full appreciation. Spring played a flute in her ear. Men who used to pass by as if she were invisible gave her a thorough, flattering glance. Looking at her reflection in the window of that boutique in which she first saw the dress, she was convinced that she would blend in the store perfectly and so smoothly walked in. The saleswoman greeted her. Was she looking for something in particular? "No, just looking," she answered.

"Didn't you purchase that dress here?"

"Yes."

"It looks marvelous on you."

The woman allowed Elizabeth to proceed with her shopping. When she reached the back of the store, Jimmy turned over and his plastic milk bottle fell, rolling a few feet in the direction of the other saleslady, who was pouring water into a coffee machine. She picked up the bottle, put it under a faucet, then dried it. "Here. What a nice quiet baby. He or she?"

"He."

"He's cute. How old?"

"A year and eight months."

"Would you like coffee?"

"No, thank you. I just wanted to see your new dresses."

"Well, they're on that rack over here. Just let us know if you need help."

So many gorgeous dresses beyond her means. She had only examined a few, rubbing the fine fabrics between her fingers, when her charade abruptly lost its energy. Either butterflies or acidity had invaded her stomach. She thanked the salesladies and left the store. As Jimmy was asleep and it was otherwise such a pleasant afternoon, she proceeded westward on 63rd, a crosstown street of distinguished architectural facades, toward the long wall that enclosed Central Park, its trees abuzz with buds. Positioning Jimmy beside an empty sidewalk bench, she took out her leather-covered notebook to study for her final exams. She turned the cover and Santa Barbara gazed at her.

Burying the saint under turned pages, she intended to start reading, but her mind drifted as the sight of Saint Barbara brought to mind her uptown bus ride, the old gray passengers gazing at her and Jimmy on the bus, the Italian fruit man who called Jimmy her baby, the spooky woman who assured that she would have her own baby, her discovering the dress on a rack in Luis's El Barrio. A seasickness tolled in her stomach again.

This time the ill-feeling persisted, resistant to antacid tablets from Mrs. Farber's medicine cabinet, and Elizabeth had to take it to the school reception, where she was cured by the pleasant distraction of her classmates. She had not cultivated many friendships, but almost all her women classmates came up to compliment how she looked and chat for a while. She was also approached by almost every one of her male classmates, among them Luis, who as usual was funny and sort of charming.

Either in his constant playfulness or inadvertently, he called her Isabel, her real given name, which surprised her, nicely of course. At the end of the reception he came up and said that because she looked as she did in that dress, he couldn't think of her taking the subway home and offered her a taxi ride to Brooklyn. She considered accepting his offer but declined, realizing only after she announced her decision how hard Luis took the rejection.

Luckily another classmate, Leonard, a chubby, balding married Jewish guy from Park Slope remembered that she too was from Brooklyn and invited to drive her home. Leonard's motives probably weren't saintly either, but he was always a gentleman, and it was true that he was heading in the same direction.

Her mother, who was anxious to hear how the evening went, had been looking out the window when Elizabeth stepped out of Leonard's car. But Elizabeth immediately defused her mother's expectations of being narrated a soap opera chapter by clarifying that her driver was a married classmate who happened to live in Brooklyn and offered to drop her off. Her mother also understood that Elizabeth was exhausted and wanted to go straight to bed.

In the dark, she tried to visualize her mother's reaction had she returned to Brooklyn accompanied by Luis. Most likely her mother would have closed her bedroom door and behaved as if she had seen nothing, but unable to contain the emotions that seethed overnight, the following morning she would have started her Inquisition. The room began to feel hot and muggy. Elizabeth turned on the light again and opened the window. A breeze blew through her nightgown, cooling her body as she admired the dress on a hanger hooked over the closet door.

She lifted the hanger from the door and, as she modeled the dress, pressed against her body, in the body-length mirror on the closet door she began to sway, dancing to an imagined *bolero*. That's what the night lacked, dancing. Gliding and dipping theatrically, she gave in to this momentary abandon, surrendering to the fantasy of wearing her dress as she danced against a background of music in a Latin setting. She really did love this dress, especially after the way Luis looked at her.

That admission petrified her. She had never dated a Latin man. The only Latin man remotely in her life had been her father. As if in a dream she frequently thought back to one of rare moments when he came to visit. He would sit his little girl on his knee and call her his little Isabel, *Isabelita*. Then at a point she couldn't fix in memory, he disappeared from her life, and the only thing she knew by heart was the reason why, as throughout her sad childhood her mother angrily vented how cowardly her father had capitulated to his selfish wife, who made him choose between her and seeing his daughter in Brooklyn.

Although he sent support money regularly until he died, her mother's bitterness never abated, and as Javier had apparently not been the first man of her culture to fail her, she extended her hatred to every Latin man, her bitterness compelling her to raise her daughter as Elizabeth, for whose sake she spoke only English even if thickly accented and moved out of neighborhoods where others of her kind were invading. Her niece Carmen, who lived with them since she had gotten divorced, provided another income so they could readily afford to move.

Five years older than Elizabeth, Carmen was a single mother who waited until her son was old enough to be left in daycare so she could work and move into her own apartment. Her reluctance to remarry seemed to be the bitter fruit of her own history much like Elizabeth's mother, and from listening to Carmen and her mother vent their feelings, Elizabeth grew up having the same lesson instilled of running from Latin men, their endemic sexual treachery, their making the women bear all the responsibilities. "It's not just the Bonjours, like I was told—it's all of them," her mother would warn repeatedly.

So when Elizabeth came home excited about the dress, Carmen didn't inquire but took for granted that her younger cousin was smitten with the only kind of man that she in her right mind would want. After all, Elizabeth had dated the right kind before and was engaged to one before his loony parents frightened the poor guy with the fear that somehow a black child would result from their union.

To be sure, Carmen's message was contradictory because she still swooned at Latin singers and movie stars and obliquely lamented that despite their ideal other qualities, *americanos* usually couldn't dance and looked sexually bland. And her mother too contradicted herself, notably with the "perfect men" from her family's side. Her own brother Esteban was supposedly a loyal husband for thirty years. Her cousin Francisco was respected by all as a religiously devote man, a posture of praise that Elizabeth believed was just family denial because it was plain as day that women terrified him. No matter how broad or inconsistent her mother's condemnation of Latin manhood, Elizabeth was supposed to know enough not to include into that morass the perfect exceptions from her mother's family.

But not one male soul from the Bonjour bloodline was forgiven. Her mother's island relations who lived in the municipal ward next to Bonjour regularly related the most recent gossip to come out of that lineage, and with relish her mother immediately passed on each latest proof of her thesis on Latin men—even more sarcastically nuanced—to Elizabeth.

As a teenager she rebelliously defended her phantom father, the father of Isabel, provoking her mother to become frighteningly incensed. Her mother would remind her that if her last name was still Bonjour, it was only to protect her from an even more ridiculous fate. "Given how those Bonjour men cast off children like pollen, what would have happened if you had met Javier's child from the Bronx or some other child he could have secretly had on the side anywhere else in this city, and neither of you knew?" She was repeating another old warning about the Bonjours.

Elizabeth was still in high school when she learned of the horrible death of her half-brother. She had often wondered about seeking him out but never got up the courage to defy her mother. Besides, what would have been the point? Edgar was just a stranger to her. Nevertheless, when she was told of Edgar's death by her mother, who brought home the newspaper with the report and the photograph, she was saddened and regretted never having followed through and gotten in touch. Of course, she didn't dare to confess this sentiment to her mother, who not only did not exactly lament but read the news account aloud as if to reaffirm with that illustration the treachery she had taught her daughter to escape.

Her father was weak, maybe cowardly, because he never stood up to his wife, but Martina was, after all, his wife, Elizabeth secretly rationalized. And no matter what redundant proof her mother could show, in Elizabeth's heart of hearts she felt that her father watched over her somehow, would come through somehow. Maybe the guilt that he made Martina feel was her proof that something good could be said for her father, and that maybe she shouldn't adhere to her mother's bitterness toward all Latin men.

The telephone rang, sounding louder at such a late hour. Before Elizabeth could pick up, the ringing stopped. She opened the door to her room and heard her mother speak to the voice on the other end. "I'll call her. What is your name?" After a pause, her mother came to her door. "It's for you. A Luis?"

The ice in her mother's tone penetrated, leaving her frozen.

"Well, do you want me to tell him that you are sleeping?"

"No, I'll talk to him. This must be something about our class work." She picked up in her room.

Luis apologized for calling so late . . .

"How did you get my number?"

"I asked the professor. Remember, he took the entire class's numbers at the beginning of the term. I told him that you had meant to give me the number at the reception but then you had to leave and forgot."

"Why did you say that?"

"Because I was afraid to ask you for the number and be turned down and because I think that it's the truth, that you really would have wanted if I asked but something would have held you back."

"What is it that you want?"

There was a long pause. She could hear her mother outside pacing, puttering, when she normally would have been sleeping at that hour. "Isn't it obvious? I couldn't take my eyes off of you tonight. I thought . . ."

She lowered her voice, "Luis, look, I would prefer not to stay on the phone right now. I'll talk tomorrow in class, okay." She hung up before he answered. She turned out the light, hoping to deter her mother, who, true to her nature, opened the bedroom door anyway.

"What did Luis want at this hour?"

"Luis had lost his class notes and called to ask me to be sure to bring my notebook so he could make a copy of my notes. Goodnight."

She almost shut the door, but then poked her head back into the room: "I was cleaning up and found the store receipt still in the Bloomingdales shopping bag. Did you need it?"

Unthinking, Elizabeth told her to throw it out, and her mother shut the door. But in seconds she remembered that the receipt stated the actual store name and address on 116th Street. She didn't sleep well worrying about that detail.

The following day Mrs. Farber asked if at all possible Elizabeth could work another week, allowing her replacement to become available. But Elizabeth had made appointments for job interviews. For the rest of the day, she tried to concentrate on studying for finals, although her mind was alternately worrying about her mother's having seen that store receipt and how to deal with Luis. She wasn't yet ready to confront the questions he was making her pose to herself while she lived with her mother. And why should she have to answer them anyway? Who was to say that her mother wasn't right?

Later that day she walked to class, and as she entered the lobby of the Hunter College building Luis happened to be standing off near a snack stand in the far corner, talking to the classmate who had driven her home the night before. She tried to get to the elevators unnoticed, preferring to talk later in the classroom, but he saw her and came over.

He immediately apologized for calling so late, and she made light of the offense. He invited her to sit for a while so he could tell her something, which was really the reason why he had called the night before, being a bit overexcited perhaps. He led the way to available seats by the snack bar, from where he offered her coffee and pastry, which she declined. He was really expressing such enthusiasm at being with her, his eyes radiating pleasure, prompting her to feel clumsy, ill-equipped, wanting to but somehow unable to respond in kind. Because he worked in a bank by day, he was wearing a blue suit and in the second that he remained standing as she sat he looked exactly like that man who had offered her his seat in the subway some days earlier.

"We only have fifteen minutes to get to class," she reminded him.

"I know, but I had to tell you this. I was talking to my mother about you—don't get nervous, I meant about your last name because it's not very common among Puerto Ricans. And she said that, and you won't believe this, my father's mother's maiden name was Bonjour. And she said that everybody on the island knows that only one family has that name. So can you believe this? We are related."

"Did she tell you anything else about the Bonjours?"

"No, what?"

"Oh, nothing, just that the one-family legend goes way back, and the Bonjours are all spread out so your grandmother's Bonjours may be very distant from my father's line. I mean we may be very, very distantly related."

"That's enough to make me happy."

There wasn't much time for more conversation, so Luis directly asked permission to call her, to date her. She answered that she would have to think about it.

And she did think about it, her attention constantly drifting from the class discussion as she wondered if she herself was rejecting Luis's interest in her or was it her mother planted inside her. At the end of the class, she asked Luis for his number because if her decision was yes, she would call him, but that he should not call her at home just yet.

From that point on, on the subway ride home, she prepared herself for an unpleasant confrontation when she got home because her mother, who that night didn't work, surely would not let the El Barrio store receipt pass unnoticed without a venting of backlogged emotions. Preparing herself, she also seriously thought that after she got a job she should live on her own or move in with Carmen, although she also knew she could not abandon her mother like that, or simply leave unmarried.

She turned the key and opened the door slowly and saw what she least expected. Her mother was sitting at the dining table in tears, profoundly distraught. At first Elizabeth thought that island relatives had called to give her bad news of somebody's death. "What happened?"

Surely whatever it was had to be something beyond words because her mother could not speak and gasped for air as if gathering great strength just to begin. She begged Elizabeth to understand what she was about to say. She had been doing the laundry and went into Elizabeth's room to get clothes that needed washing. She saw that lovely dress and noticed that it had a little stain from last night. "Maybe you didn't see it in the night, but I wanted to do you a favor, and I thought I would clean out the stain."

Painfully she narrated that had started brushing the stain lightly with a little detergent on a moist cloth. This was over the washing machine that was full of whites. Because her mind was distracted by something, she didn't know how it happened, her hand slipped so the cloth she was using fell into the water. Forgetting that she had already poured bleach in the water, she picked the cloth out of the water and started to brush again. The stain came out but so did the dress's color, forming a white spot. And there were bleached spots everywhere on which the cloth had dropped water or touched the dress.

"It's ruined. I'm so sorry. I couldn't bear to have you see it, so I threw it out. I'll take you to Bloomingdales and we'll find you another one, a better one. I am so sorry, Elizabeth, please, please forgive me for being so stupid and clumsy."

The Inheritance

1

Gabriel Bonjour opened his eyes and realized that he was still at the steering wheel of his father's beat-up van. He had parked in the airport lot intending to take the shuttle bus and see whether Miguel had caught a late flight or had passed out and was sleeping off his drunken rage. But once parked, he stopped to ask himself if it was worthwhile to chase after Miguel. He shut his eyes for what he thought would be a moment, but the long crazy day took its toll, and he fell into a deep sleep. When he awoke, he remained in a stupor, staring at the single twinkling star in the windshield until he remembered why he was parked at the airport. It was almost midnight. The airlines had certainly all closed their counters by now . . .

2

When Aunt Lucy telephoned that Julián had suffered a massive stroke and wasn't expected to see the morning, Gabriel's sympathy for her expression of loss was the closest thing to grief he could summon up. Lucy urged him that the right thing was for him to fly down that evening. His wife Sandra agreed. She pointed out to him that, it being Wednesday, except for two workdays before the weekend he had little else to lose, but if he didn't go to the funeral he might regret that decision for the rest of his life. Gabriel then conferred with Mami Blanca, who reminded him that Julián was, for good or ill, his father, but added that he should do what he felt in his heart. Not sure what that was, he listened to Sandra, made the flight reservation, then called Lucy to tell her that he would be arriving late. In less than two hours he was standing at an airlines counter shelling out more cash in ten seconds than his father had spent on him in twenty-nine years.

At the airport bar, he downed a double scotch that he hoped would make him nod off once he was on board, and the scotch did the trick. The next time he awoke the stewardess was leaning over to check that his seatbelt was properly fastened for the landing. At the San Juan airport, as he waited for his suitcase, he heard his name paged to the airline counter. At that late hour, the seventy-year-old Aunt Lucy was waiting for him accompanied by his cousin Salvador.

Lucy's crush on Julián went back decades and didn't diminish even after her youngest sister Blanca married, then divorced him for being a womanizer she would never take back. So when Lucy hugged Gabriel, her embrace encompassed two men. She whispered in his ear, "*Ya murió.* He's gone. But I knew you would come. You had to. No matter what may have happened in life, he was your father." She stepped back, bit her lower lip, staring at him intensely. "Your sad black eyes are his, that entire family's."

Gabriel had heard those words countless times while growing up, and they always rang ironic because Mami Blanca had raised him to lose every vestige of the Bonjours. Except for his surname, he was really a Márquez, and being with his aunts Lucy and Mariana, who spoiled him shamelessly, was the Paradise to which he often dreamed of returning from distant New York City. Five other aunts figured in the array of Márquez daughters, but the two eldest were his surrogate grandmothers, replacing his real ones, who both died before he was born.

Lucy and Mariana, in fact, had practically raised their littlest sister, his Mami Blanca, who didn't share their old ways of surviving island men. Her older sisters, she once explained to her son, belonged to a time when women were brought up to endure many things that they considered inherent masculine defects, accepting inevitable betrayal rather than losing social respectability. They pleaded with her that she be more flexible and practical, but she was too independent to listen. She divorced Julián, then left with their baby Gabriel, joining the planeloads that were leaving for New York, to live with their widowed middle-aged sister Clemencia.

Up north Blanca had nothing more to do with the Bonjour family, so everything Gabriel knew about them had percolated through his mother's relentless indoctrination against their genealogy. Privately, however, there blossomed in him a secret hobby of keeping track of migrant Bonjours, a curiosity that he was able to satisfy thanks to the lore his mother passed on to him that only one island family possessed his surname and that every Bonjour he would ever meet would be blood kin. Knowing this, every year when a new telephone directory came out, he looked up how many more Bonjours had settled in New York. In some years he had stumbled on "Bonjour, Julián" but didn't mention it to Mami Blanca. Over the years the list had grown to over twenty relatives, whom he often thought of calling but never did. Now, at a funeral parlor, he would be discovering the continent of his unknown lineage and seeing some of the faces whose names he had seen in the phone book.

Salvador dropped off Lucy and Gabriel in front of her house, where visible in the dining room window was Aunt Mariana. Her eyes were full of tears, but she became gleeful at the sight of Gabriel. Before touching him, she asked him to wait, signaling with her open hand. Now totally deaf, she needed to slip in the hearing aid that she had finally agreed to wear but that more often remained on the dining table. The aid in place, she came alive, as if hearing gave her sight, and she saw him for the first time. She embraced him, "*Ay, estoy triste, Gabby.* I am sad, Gabby. He was a good man. When she lived on the island with him, Blanca never lacked for a thing, and she never needed to work. He felt betrayed that she left for New York and took you from him; he was so hurt and never wanted to look back. That's why he abandoned you. I tried to explain to Blanca to reconsider, but . . . And he was a man who would help whoever asked or needed. He helped me and my husband and was the kind of person who never came by to be repaid. His trust in you made you repay. That's how he was to people he liked. He had his weaknesses, I know, but he had his honorable side. And he was the handsomest man . . ." This from Mariana, whose husband lived and died a drunk, and who subsequently spoke of men as the cross that women were given to carry. But she never had a maligning word for Julián Bonjour. Logically, also spared from that corrupt genetic scheme was Gabriel, for whose sake she abandoned her reflex solidarity with women.

Sitting at the dining table, the two aunts sighed with sad resignation to Julián's passing until Lucy asked Gabriel about his new wife, if she was in good health. What they really wanted to know was if she was going to give him a child. They were skeptical about her inability thus far to get herself pregnant. Was she, like his first wife, too "modern" for such essential things? Mariana reminded him yet again that he wasn't getting any younger. When he was married to his previous wife, Mariana one day whispered to him, "If that woman doesn't want to give you a child, have one on the side, and we'll raise it for you."

As Lucy reminded him yet again about the importance of having children who would look after him in his old age, Gabriel mentally stepped back and observed the two old women. Age brought out their contrasting qualities. Mariana, younger by two years, in fact looked older. She was pale and washed out, grown overcautious, frail, with complete disregard for vanity, wearing her short hair pinned back at the sides. The deeply etched waves of her brow, the sagging pouches under her eyes, and the line of her lips all arced downward, like the tilt of her head, the attitude of her eyes, and her drooping breasts. Beside her, Lucy could easily be taken for several years her junior. She wore a steel-enforced bra, her hair brightly tinted and in a bun always colored by a ribbon. Makeup partly covered her wrinkles, or maybe she just had fewer than her sister, and she was blessed with the smile of a young girl.

But the sharply contrasting two women spoke as one in reporting how lucky his cousin Lucho was to have his two daughters comfort him with their love and devotion while he died of cancer, and Lucho's sense of accomplishment that he had raised them to be such great ladies. Both the daughters went to college, raised their children, then went on to become lawyers. Finally, it was Mariana who fell out of step to apologize for subjecting him to their lecture, forgetting why he had flown down, and that he needed to sleep.

In bed, Gabriel listened to the sweet racket of tree frogs that loudly whistled *coquí, coquí* in the humid night. A pale moonlight entered through the open shutter window. His thoughts hived, wondering how things were back in New York. His wife said she would call in at Lincoln Hospital, where he was an X-ray technician, and let his supervisor know he would be out for the rest of the week. Luckily he had accumulated some sick days. He took a deep breath, tasted the special flavor of Caribbean night air. This was good, but except for the pleasure of seeing his aunts, he really hated having to return to this hick hole of an island. He had outgrown its romantic spell and small town attitudes, turned off by his having always been made to feel stupid because he spoke such a mangled Spanish and because everyone always asked why, being almost thirty, he didn't yet have a family. This used to be his Paradise, but now he would rather be back in New York, where it was late spring and the hockey season was ending and the Rangers were battling their way for a berth in the Stanley Cup playoffs.

He intended that to be his final words to himself for the night, but closing his eyes did not bring on sleep. He thought of Julián. Mariana and Lucy had spoken about him before, but Gabriel had never paid attention. And now their grief, their expression of true love for him suddenly provoked an unexpected sadness, a sorrow that came from his realizing that he had always mistakenly assumed that lives didn't just end in tattered loose ends, that at some imaginary point, Julián would return to make amends, fill in the hungry gaps of his son's life story. Now, realizing that things do remain in futile pieces forever, he suddenly desired to know his father, the entire package of his Bonjour blood, that mysterious side of himself.

3

Clemencia's apartment in the Bronx was the gloomiest place for Mami Blanca to have arrived from Paradise to start a new life. The building was a blocked letter C closed in by the windowless wall of an adjoining public school. Clemencia lived in the building's sunless rear half, facing the back windows of the apartments fortunate enough to look out on the street. Near sunset every day, some sunlight entered Clemencia's kitchen and living room windows, which otherwise looked out at the school wall and a descending crisscross of gray clothes lines over the meaningless courtyard five flights below, a playground for vermin. The clotheslines' geometric designs provided a form of entertainment for the little boy Gabriel, who spent hours looking out, sometimes watching the women, their heads severed from view by the shoulder-high frame of the open window, while their tentacle arms and hands affixed dripping articles of clothing with wooden pins. The weight of each new article lengthened the sag of festooned laundry.

His only other view of the world, from Clemencia's two bedroom windows, was forbidden. Whatever light naturally shone on those windows was kept out by a shade always pulled down over the lattice of two collapsible, steel security gates. Beyond the gates, the windows faced the backs of the buildings on a street they never walked down owing to its being inhabited by *los morenos,* which meant black *americanos.*

During the week, as he was still too young for kindergarten, while Clemencia and Mami Blanca sewed at the same factory, Gabriel spent his days with Cuca, a neighbor in their building who made a living caring for numerous children, and whose second-floor window faced the street. Like him, all the children who played with him at Cuca's house were brought there and taken home by husbandless mothers. And because Cuca herself, always on the telephone with her girlfriends, often discussed the problem of men, Gabriel spent the better part of his day looking out the window for his mother to come home from work and thinking about how bad Julián was and how much he never ever wanted to be like him.

But such recurring thoughts sometimes also made him miss his father, whom Gabriel imagined knocking on Cuca's door and picking him up, out of the blue, to take him to the park. He harbored that dream because on a couple of occasions, when he was littler,

Julián moved to New York and once or twice showed up one evening unannounced at Clemencia's. Otherwise in those days his visits were always on weekends, when Mami Blanca didn't have to go to work. In the morning she would tell him that his Papi was coming later that day. As *later* meant nothing to him, Gabriel expected him any minute, but he was soon able to figure out when the time was near because just before Julián would arrive Mami Blanca always got dressed up. Not like when she got herself ready for a party, but she looked pretty. Also on those days Aunt Clemencia passed the morning giving Mami Blanca solemn advice on what to tell him about the support money she was owed. Just before he arrived, Clemencia always went off somewhere.

Those visits followed a pattern. He wore a suit and a great smile. He would lift Gabriel in his arms and carry him to the sofa. Mami Blanca would say hello and follow them into the living room. Julián rarely brought anything for Gabriel. One Christmas, he brought a gift, a Dick Tracy toy car, but he only came for Christmas once. Other times he didn't bring anything, just his wide smile and black wavy hair. Gabriel would play with Julián's fat fingers while his parents conversed seriously over his head.

Julián never ate anything at Clemencia's. Mami Blanca never offered anything to eat or drink. Sometimes Julián mounted him on his knee to ride horsey. Once Gabriel heard Julián say that he was a travel agent, words that Gabriel didn't understand. But the time Gabriel was never to forget was one afternoon when Julián said that he had to leave. As his father hadn't stayed very long, Gabriel started to cry. Julián promised that he would be right back, that he was only going downstairs to get him ice cream. Gabriel waited at the door, but years would pass before he saw that smile and wavy hair again.

4

Julián's wake was being held at Otto Marín's Casa Funeraria in the town of Vega Alta, where he was born and where he would be buried. Félix Bonjour, Gabriel's uncle, called Lucy to find out if Julián's son had arrived and to request a favor. Things were, as one could well imagine, hectic on the Bonjour side owing to the preparations that must be made, so Félix asked if Gabriel could be dropped off at Julián's widow's house, where a family member would go by to take them to the funeral parlor.

Lucy and Mariana persuaded the reluctant Gabriel that he should get to know the widow, Angelina, considering the solemnity of the occasion and the years that have passed. His aunts regretted that as much as they would have wanted to attend the wake, they no longer drove, and neither of their children could take the entire day off from work to drive them there and back. They promised to say a rosary for him and light a candle in church. Mariana's son, René, drove Gabriel to the widow's house.

Julián had lived on the third floor of a modest four-story pink building with white balconies. Gabriel rang downstairs. *"Hola, hola,"* he heard from the third floor balcony. He looked up to see a short, plump woman leaning over and looking down. *"Yo soy Gabriel."* Angelina became exuberant, "Gabriel, *hijo, que Dios lo bendiga.* Gabriel, child, God bless you. Here catch this key and open the gate." The key was on a chain with a large Plexiglas photo holder that contained a two-inch long color reproduction of a blond Jesus looking out a window as a ray of light shown on his face. When Gabriel reached the third floor, Angelina was waiting at the top of the stairs. She embraced him as if she had known him all his life.

He had expected a *negra* because that was how Mami Blanca and Clemencia identified her throughout his life. "Ever since your father took up with that *negra* . . . ," they would say in Spanish. But this Angelina, who led him into her apartment door wasn't dark and, except for black hair that was somewhat frizzy, her features were not readily identifiable as black. And even though he had been trained to dislike her, her obvious mourning behind a cheerful attitude inspired sympathy: her eyes were wet and red, and around her neck she wore a rosary. After hearing Gabriel's first stumbling words in Spanish, she politely switched to a West Indian–accented English, "My God, you are the image of Julián. Look at those eyes, my god. Come in, come in." Mami Blanca once said that Angelina was originally Puerto Rican but raised on St. Thomas.

In the center of the small, bright living room cramped with old wooden and cloth furniture stood a stout young black man with a closely shaved head. He wore a dark blue work shirt and pants, the kind car mechanics wear, both grease-soiled. His hands and arms, exposed by rolled up sleeves, were also darkened by the residue of grease. Angelina introduced her son, "Gabriel, this is Miguel, your brother. I'm sorry you have to meet now like this."

Miguel didn't smile and just extended a dead hand. "If it were up to me, I wouldn't be here," he snapped in a deep, African American voice and walked off toward the balcony. Angelina, embarrassed, invited Gabriel to sit in a rocking chair sofa, Julián's favorite he was told. She offered him a rum and Coke, which he accepted. As she was in the kitchen preparing the *Cuba libre,* he stood up and took an inventory of his father's living room: a large television set, a cabinet with knickknacks, old furniture. On the wall a black and white photograph of Julián and Angelina showed how comely she had looked decades earlier. Her hourglass figure filled out a calf-length dress, and she wore a hat, like a sequined half-moon, with feathers protruding from both ends.

That photo hung between two others. To its left was a color shot of a very pretty girl with the fairest skin and the blackest eyes and almost blue hair, and on the right, a black-and-white high school graduation portrait of a black male teenager wearing a mortarboard, with his dark ears sticking out against a white backdrop, gown, and mortarboard. But the girl, a young lady really, was so exceptionally striking that Gabriel got up to take a closer look at her picture.

He was standing in front of it when Angelina returned with a tray with glasses, a bottle of rum, a can of Coke, a dish of lime slices. "That's my daughter, Angie, from another marriage. She's coming down with her kids. Julián raised her like his own. Miguel is supposed to pick her up at the airport tomorrow morning and drive her to the burial." She looked over to Miguel, with his hands on the balcony rails as he stared at the sky.

Angelina placed the tray on the glass coffee table in front of the sofa and sat under the pictures. As she prepared him the drink, Gabriel leaned back in the rocker, contemplating his father's widow. In her grief, needing to vindicate Julián to his son, she assured Gabriel that he was constantly in Julián's thoughts and that his father wished so much that things had been different, but he knew how much Blanca wanted her life without him in it. Her voice remained low, her eyes vigilant of the balcony, where Miguel was now fidgeting, pounding the palm of his hand on the balcony railing. His puffy hands, as well as the slouch of his shoulders, were exactly like their father's.

Angelina had stopped talking to observe Gabriel looking at Miguel. Sensing his curiosity about his half-brother, she called Miguel to join them, but he either didn't hear her or paid no attention. She whispered to Gabriel, "I really don't want him to drink."

Gabriel himself had nervously downed two drinks, maybe reacting to Miguel's pounding or to the sight of Angelina, at once the beautiful woman in the photograph of more than forty years ago and the woman who stole his father, who was now delivering the words of paternal love that his father never spoke himself. The rum relaxed him, allowed him to listen to her expressions of grief interwoven with reassurances that his father always wished to be closer to his distant son. In this rum-relaxed state, he pointed to the wall behind her and commented to Angelina that her daughter was beautiful.

"Julián adored her. He raised her like his own . . . ," Angelina repeated, suddenly stricken by grief. She pulled a handkerchief out of a pocket in her housedress and blew her nose. It was a man's handkerchief, doubtless one of Julián's, with a purple border. "He had always been stubborn and felt it was you who should have sought out your father, no matter what Blanca thought. Those were his values." Unloading those feelings caused her to cry again, this time uncontrollably. After regaining her composure, she blew her nose again. "He was stubborn, just plain stubborn. I told him to call you. I told him to see the doctor about those headaches, but he never listened to nobody, to nobody . . ."

Miguel stepped into the living room and announced that their ride to the funeral parlor was parking in front. His wide body seemed crowded in by the furniture. He leaned over and poured himself an inch of straight rum. Angelina asked him to just have one.

"Do you see what I'm drinking?" he asked Gabriel, raising his index finger, "One."

Downstairs, a car horn honked twice. Angelina went out to the balcony and waved to someone down on the street. "Gabriel, we have to go."

"I need money." Miguel's voice was a contained roar.

"I'll pay you for gas later."

"You pay me now, Moms. You don't know this woman, man, she gets her way, she gets what she wants and makes you pay for it." He smiled, Julián's smile. "I didn't have no money to come down here. I told you that. You needed this show, then you pay for it. Man never gave me nothing, no love, no money, nothing but grief." Julián's pudgy, curled index finger, hammering downward, emphasized every negative point.

She took some rolled bills out of her pocketbook and placed them on the coffee table. "Can you please change those clothes for the funeral?"

"I didn't bring no clothes, you know that, and I don't care what the fuck those people say. I'm just a grease monkey, okay, that's me. No college, nothing."

"Your father's clothes fit you. You know where they are."

The car honked twice again. Angelina removed her car keys from a purse and left them for Miguel on the coffee table. "Please don't drink anymore today. Gabriel, come."

Gabriel extended his hand, about to say he was glad to have finally met his brother, but Miguel was too absorbed staring at his mother and didn't see the hand. At the door, Angelina turned around and reminded Miguel that he had to pick up his sister at the American Airlines terminal at ten o'clock that night. She said this pointing to the rum bottle. Miguel picked up the bottle. "No problem. No problem." Angelina stared at him, warning him with her eyes as she began to close the door. But before it shut, there was an explosive shatter of glass. She flung the door open to discover a huge wet stain against the wall by the door frame and shattered glass on the floor. Miguel stood in the middle of the living room with his hands on his hips. He addressed his mother in his contained roar, "What? What? Not another drink."

5

At the funeral home, Gabriel's unexpected presence seemed to please the entire Bonjour clan, unanimously relieved that Julián can truly rest knowing that both his sons would be present at his funeral. In every Bonjour, he was able to identify a bodily feature in common with his father: a cousin Jose's plump cheeks, an aunt Wilma's charming smile, an uncle Frank's balding wavy hair. Bonjour traits packed the funeral hall.

Angelina led Gabriel by the hand to the casket so he could say farewell. Standing alone on the raised platform, he looked back at the rows of mourners and at Angelina, smiling pleased, a few steps away. He felt foolish standing before Julián's waxed-looking dead face. He had not seen that face in almost five years, and the prospect of not seeing it ever again simply evoked feelings not much different than the prospect of seeing him in another decade. He neither loved nor hated the man. He leaned over, kissed his forehead and whispered, "I'm sorry it never worked out."

6

Gabriel spent the night at the funeral parlor, where, as a chorus of women prayed all night to the Virgin Mary, he made small talk with the younger Bonjours and eventually caught a few hours of sleep on a couch in the foyer. The following morning he rode with Angelina in the slow procession of cars to the gates of Vega Alta's small, weedy town cemetery with packed-in grave sites. For the duration of that short trip, Angelina expressed her concern that Angie might not make it to the burial because of Miguel.

At the cemetery gate, Gabriel was expected to be one of eight pallbearers. The morning had not been exceptionally hot, but the burial started after eleven, in the fast-peaking tropical sun in which the sweat-soaked bearers had to lead the trailing mourners to a family plot somewhere up ahead through a maze of soot-darkened gravestones. Angelina walked beside Gabriel, on whose padded shoulder rested a rear corner of the casket. Surrounding voices asked Angelina for Angie and Miguel, and she explained that they were due any minute.

The casket was set down on the concrete base around the rectangular metal covering of an underground crypt. Two cemetary workers removed the crypt's cover. As Gabriel stared into the cold, damp space already occupied with the piled caskets of other Bonjours he never knew, four broad cloth straps were aligned in parallel rows over the opening, and the two cemetery laborers descended into the crypt. When Gabriel looked up and panned the mourners gathered around, his eyes fell on a young woman consoling Angelina, who was weeping uncontrollably. From the photograph, he recognized Angie, who was also crying, sniffling into a tissue as her other arm embraced her mother.

A priest stepped out of the crowd, onto the base of the crypt, and waited for silence that came soon so he could begin the formalities and read a prayer from a little book. When he finished, a thin bony man with high cheekbones and greasy hair combed straight back identified himself as a friend and offered a few words "to remind us of Julián's generosity, his willingness to help others at any time." He was certain that God had already welcomed Julián to the heavenly kingdom.

While this man eulogized, Gabriel couldn't keep his eyes off Angie, her eyes covered by white-framed circular sunglasses. She looked even more attractive than her photograph. She was short and shapely, and against her black dress and black hair, her skin seemed smoothly milkier than in the picture, and her painted lips extremely red, with a natural, sensual pout about them. He compared her to a photo of his Mami Blanca at that age, a girl who was pretty, thin and ladylike. If Angie was any true reflection of Angelina's magnetism in her youth, Gabriel understood a little why Julián lost his head.

The bearers were asked to approach the casket. Imitating the others, Gabriel stepped up to the crypt cover, grabbed an end of the parallel strap and passed it behind his back. Bending down as the bearers were doing in unison, with one hand in front and one behind, he gripped the strap to raise the casket, position it over the opening, and then loosen his grip to let it slowly descend into the tomb, where the two cemetery laborers inside the crypt positioned it over another casket. Gabriel stared at the casket amid mourners who passed around him to throw a flower into the open crypt. He kept staring until the last flower was thrown, and as the laborers who had climbed out pushed the metal lid, the final curtain on his lifelong wait for Julián.

The unceremonious return of mourners to their cars branched out in streaming paths between the tombstones. Gabriel caught up to Angelina, still walking under the arm of Angie, who gave him a half-smile as she pressed his hand.

When they reached the car, in the shade of a wide tree, Miguel was asleep at the driver's seat, and in the back seat dozed Angie's baby and toddler. Angie opened the rear door, and Miguel awoke and sat up, saying nothing. Angelina, obviously trying to avoid confrontation, tugged at Gabriel to move on ahead to ride in the car that had brought them.

Angelina was in better shape by the time they got to the family gathering at the house of Aunt Wilma, whom Gabriel had met at the funeral parlor. Wilma, a gray-haired woman with Julián's robust smile, lived closest to the cemetery and was already home when everybody got to her place. At her door, she embraced Gabriel in tears because this lost nephew was "the picture of my brother!" When she released him, she informed Angelina that Angie had arrived just minutes before and was tending to her baby in one of the bedrooms, but that Miguel never even got out of the car. Angelina expressed no reaction and offered to help Wilma serve the food. Gabriel was told to feel at home, to mingle with his Bonjour relations out on the carport.

As soon as he stepped outside, a cousin about his own age called him over. He was Victor, a lawyer whom he had met the night before. Victor presented Gabriel to his two brothers, one a bank teller, who had flown in from New York that morning, and the other a croupier at the Hilton casino. The two brothers reminded him that, even though they had just met, he was blood and to call on them at anytime for anything. Other introductions followed with other clusters of relations. At some point, an auburn-haired, fortyish cousin named Teresa, who ran her own decorating business in San Diego, came up to him and gave him her card. If he were to visit San Diego, she promised to pick him up at the airport.

By this time Wilma had served lunch on plastic plates, and Gabriel ate, taking discreet glances at Angie, who had come outside to eat among a circle of women. When he finished his meal, Angelina offered to get him more salad, chicken, more pork, or anything else, but he was fine. She asked him how it felt being among so many Bonjours. He felt okay, he answered. She gave him a glance that reminded him of how much he looked like Julián and then surprised him by expressing her regret that he was still childless. "I think you should work on that before it is too late. Time passes faster than you think. I keep telling my Angie that. She's a great mother. But her husband doesn't deserve her, and I think that she's at the point of leaving him. Stupid guy, look at that beauty. So many men don't know what is good for them."

Gabriel asked her why Miguel hadn't stayed. Staring off into the sun-bleached afternoon, she explained that her son hated these family gatherings, but that she could understand his feelings. A sudden look on her face told him that his asking about his brother gave her an idea. "Miguel has to drive to Ponce, you know, to the southern coast, tomorrow to deliver a motorcycle that Julián had sold. I need that money to help pay for the funeral. Maybe you could accompany him so he wouldn't have to take that long trip alone, and it would be a good way for you both to get to know each other." Gabriel didn't agree but didn't decline and turned the conversation to Angie. He told Angelina that he wanted to keep in touch with her in New York. Angie had a new number, so Angelina took him to where she was sitting. Angie had removed the sunglasses and her eyes could now be read although they said very little. "Sure, of course," she said, and wrote the number on a cover she tore from a book of matches.

Gabriel asked Angie where she lived in New York. Angie said she lived on the Upper West Side, near Columbia Presbyterian Hospital.

Gabriel, looking for any approach to her, mentioned that he worked in Lincoln Hospital in the Bronx. She asked how he was feeling, an inquiry that Gabriel interpreted as her appreciation of how questionably Julián had performed as his father. Gabriel answered honestly that he really didn't know how he felt. He was about to return the question to her but she was drying her eye with a tissue. "He was more like my real father, my only father."

7

Once when Gabriel was twelve, in a fit of cynicism his aunt Clemencia let Gabriel know what no adult had ever told him: "You know you have a brother by that *negra*. That's what they say, but we haven't seen him."

That was the second time he had heard about having a brother. When he was nine, his cousin Ricky made a crack about Gabriel's having a black brother. This happened in haughty Aunt Carmela's big house in the colonial part of San Juan. Her husband Juan, who cared for Gabriel like a blood nephew, owned several businesses and was an influential politician. Part of his summers Gabriel stayed at Carmela and Juan's house, where one Saturday morning Gabriel woke up, and Carmela was in her living room having a hushed conversation with some woman. People always came around asking Carmela for help with the government bureaucracy, and she devoted her mornings to receiving people that needed her husband's help. Gabriel therefore thought nothing of this woman in conference with Carmela and never even looked at her in fact. He went about the house looking for Ricky, who was not in his room.

He found Ricky running back into the house from the long arched foyer at the end of which, on the sidewalk, the bright sun made a silhouette of a little boy. As Ricky ran past Gabriel he laughingly said, "That black kid is your brother." Gabriel looked down the hall at the faceless silhouette. The figure shyly took a step to the side and out of sight. The encounter was so unmomentous and fleeting that Gabriel didn't believe Ricky, who ran off giggling, responding to the call of his older sister, who insisted they both sit and eat the breakfast that she had just served. Neither Ricky nor anybody else ever mentioned the boy again.

Now as he waited on Avenida De Diego in the shade of a movie marquis, Gabriel reminisced about those two other times that Miguel came up in his life. He was already twenty minutes late, if he was coming at all because Gabriel wasn't sure if he would ever see Miguel again and wasn't sure if maybe it was better if he didn't show up. The early cool had begun its surrender to the onslaught of midday heat. Gabriel started to walk down the block for something to drink when across the street a rusting, clattering red van pulled over and honked. Miguel waved from the open window.

He parked the van by a fire hydrant, stepped out and extended his hand. He explained that he'd had a rough night and had gotten up late. Bloodshot eyes backed up his story. His tone was mellower than the day before. Both his clean khaki pants and pale blue short-sleeved shirt had to be Julián's. Before they reached the first traffic light, Miguel also apologized for the previous day's tantrum with the bottle. He smiled Julián's smile. "It had nothing to do with you, man. It was just that everybody was making a big deal over the guy. He had dragged me and Moms from New York to PR and then back again whenever he felt like it, changing his mind at everybody else's expense, avoiding who knows what troubles."

Miguel hated to hear how much everybody loved the guy, neighbors, debtors, victims. "Everybody loved the guy, man, and he didn't love nobody." He sniffled, then laughed.

The van seemed to almost dismantle itself with the slightest bump or crack on the road. In the back was a Harley-Davidson that was secured from tilting by ropes tied to the van's inner ribs, although its poor suspension system kept the tied-down Harley dancing in one spot. Fortunately, light traffic permitted them to soon be riding on smooth highway.

Once on the highway, as if responding to questions that Gabriel had asked, Miguel began to relate the story of his life. He used to be a Marine, then left the service and went to work as a truck mechanic. He lives in Georgia now. His wife is also black, something that caused Julián to disown him. "I'm black. That's it, man. I can't do a fucking thing about that. What the fuck did he expect me to do. Calls my wife that *negra*. She hated his ass and the whole Bonjour family. She didn't want me to come down, no way. The Bonjours are a bunch of phony shits. They never really wanted us, me or my Moms. They always talked about what a fine lady your mom is."

Gabriel listened, sympathizing but tongue-tied. He imagined Julián's cruelty with Miguel, having seen it at work with others, including himself. Gabriel needed to get to know Miguel better, seeing himself in his brother's pain.

"Gabriel, did you know we might have an older brother? They say he's very sick." Gabriel didn't know.

"You didn't? Pops swore up and down that guy wasn't his, but I never believed a word that man said. Anyway, I never saw him. Don't even know where he lives. Uncle Celestino once let it slip out when we got drunk together."

They stopped at a roadside store for munchies and sodas. Miguel caught Gabriel observing the pint bottles of rum and encouraged him. "Go ahead. I had enough last night, and I'll be doing the driving." Miguel was only in the mood for pineapple juice, which would go with Gabriel's rum.

Stocked up with ice, drinks, snacks, they hit the road southbound and by noon were on the Caribbean half of the island, where a drought had scorched the hilly landscape. Miguel asked Gabriel to talk about himself because "You're a thin dude, man, but, you look so much like a skinny Pops. When you walked into my mom's house, I didn't like you at all." Gabriel described himself as having grown up in the Bronx, that he was an X-ray technician, and that he was married.

"Any little Juliáns around?"

Miguel found it surprising that he was childless. Miguel had two boys and a girl, but Julián didn't pay them any attention. "But how come you don't have kids?" Gabriel told him it was a long story not worth going into.

"Well, are you fucking around? You're a Bonjour, so no use lying to me. I'm one. I know."

That flippant remark poked a dormant wound in Gabriel. To

change the subject, he almost asked about Angie but quickly in-
tuited that she too would be a dangerous topic. Miguel asked Gabriel if he was aware that Julián had purchased a *cafetín* just before
he died. "It was a lunch business, and somebody worked it for him.
I don't know much about it myself except that my Moms was pissed
off that he got it. She wanted him to just call in his social security
and take it easy, but you know Pops. He always had to hustle, and he
didn't listen to nobody. Then he started feeling tired, talked of selling it. He was in the process of selling that business when he had the
stroke. Moms swears she's stuck with nothing but debts, but I know
her. She hasn't said a word about that deal, so I think Pops had already sold it. Now try to get the money from her. Slick. Slick, all
right. This piece of shit," he looked around the noisy van's ragged
interior, "is our inheritance, man."

After nearly an hour on the road, they were coming to the out-
skirts of Ponce. Miguel asked Gabriel if he had been in military
service. During the end of the Vietnam War, Gabriel was a student
at Bronx Community College, and afterward his number was
pretty high in the draft lottery. Miguel was drafted but just missed
going to Vietnam, the war being over by the time he was ready to
go. In the service he specialized in getting laid. "I weighed a lot less
then . . ."

As Miguel talked on, the pineapple and rum relaxed Gabriel a bit,
and he found himself laughing full-heartedly at Miguel's military
stories, about the great times he had with black *americanas* he met in
the South. That was how he came to marry one. Being slightly high
and listening absorbed in his brother's mannerisms, his style, his
eyes, which all reminded him of Julián, Gabriel didn't realize that the
telling of those stories was having an effect on the teller. For imbed-
ded somewhere in the account of this one particular woman, whom
he met and hit it off with, hot and sweet, was the pain sown by Julián's violent reaction that his son was a *negro* and he was going to
marry a *negra*.

Realizing late the change in Miguel, Gabriel backtracked to recover the tone of this more serious ongoing narration. "My wife
didn't want me to come down, no way. So I'm going to catch shit

when I get back, I know that. He hated me, hated me 'cause I came out black. Like my Mom's mother. That's why Angie was his favorite, and she wasn't even his own blood." Miguel stopped talking. He was crying inside. He had been crying all his life.

8

Clemencia had spent Christmas week with the family on the island, and when she got back to New York she told Mami Blanca that while shopping at the Plaza de Las Americas mall she had bumped into "the *negra* who took Julián away from you." Apparently she and Julián had married each other for the second time. Clemencia observed that Angelina wasn't a shadow of the young woman who seduced Julián away. Now she was chubby and frumpy. She told Clemencia that she and Julián were living in the Bronx, where he had bought a bar. She asked Clemencia to please pass on to Gabriel their home address and phone number, as well as the address of Julián's bar, urging that he be told that his father always thinks about him. Clemencia gave Gabriel the information only because "after all, he *is* your father, and you are a grown man and can make your own decisions."

Gabriel, a student at Bronx Community College, took several weeks to decide if he would go to see Julián. During spring break, he finally decided and simply showed up at the bar. Despite certain flashy touches—the jukebox, the pinball machine, the ample space for dancing—the Longwood Bar was homey and attracted mainly quiet, lonely people with nowhere else to spend their time. The surrounding neighborhood consisted of warehouses with a few gloomy residential buildings that provided the bar with customers.

His father now seemed shorter, had put on weight and lost much of his hair. At first he didn't recognize his son, who had sprouted into a young man. In a few seconds, though, he extended his luxuriant smile and gave him a firm *abrazo*. Gabriel was then introduced to the three barmaids, black *americanas,* who were given instructions that he should not be charged for what he consumed. He was also proudly introduced to the bar's regulars, all black, who returned the compliment by praising Julián to the high heavens as an honorable, intelligent, decent man who ran an honest, clean establishment. Their praise was only partly toadying because they also had reason to appreciate this oasis without violence in a neighborhood crawling with a gamut of drug hustles whose main offices were the other local bars.

Throughout the night Gabriel tried to comprehend his father's Spanish over the loudness of the jukebox, and Julián demonstrated that he was very pleased that Gabriel had found his way to the bar. His wife Angelina had told him of running into Clemencia and since then he wondered if his son would come around. He asked about Gabriel's mother and her sisters. He sent the warmest regards to Lucy and Mariana.

But the freshness of the encounter wore off soon, and beyond the opening formalities there was little to keep their conversation going. Gabriel asked how Julián acquired the bar. His father related in detail, with a sense of accomplishment, how he had gotten it dirt cheap from an acquaintance in the grips of some financial problems, and how he had picked up the chairs and stools at an auction. The investment was paying off, but the personal cost of security was high: he had to sleep on a cot in the back room, packing a shotgun.

He was about to describe a representative incident when one of the barmaids called his attention to the door, where a skinny black man stood carrying a small box that contained something that seemed heavier than he could hold very long. Julián went over to see what the man wanted. After a few seconds, he led the man into a back room, beckoning to Gabriel.

Inside, the man put down the box on a table. He held open the flaps to reveal a postage meter machine. The man's hands and arms trembled nervously, and he slumped at the shoulders. He sniffed and panted anxiously as he asked for twenty bucks. Julián sneered at the machine and started to walk off.

"Come on Mr. B., come on, man."

Julián stood at the door to the room and shouted to the barmaid instructions with what to do with some glasses. At his back, the man broke down to ten. Julián took a step and gestured to Gabriel to leave the room, and the desperate man followed them.

"Mr. B., I'm trying to do some business here. Come on, give me a break, man."

Julián went back to his table and held up Gabriel's glass as he instructed the barmaid to prepare his son another.

"Okay, okay. Five bucks."

The deal was sealed at five bucks.

When the man left, Julián underscored that Gabriel appreciate the kind of sacrifices he has had to make to keep his business operating. He said something more about its bringing in good money, and there was some reference to Gabriel which he couldn't understand because throughout this monologue the jukebox was now playing ever so loud that Gabriel had to read his father's lips.

Gabriel started coming around once a week. When not trying to listen to Julián speak, mainly about himself, against the din of the jukebox ("I can't lower it—that's how the customers like it"), Gabriel sat at the bar chatting with the barmaids, drinking slowly until he got high and it seemed as if he had put in enough time so he could leave.

Fortunately his first wife understood that he needed his father and gave him latitude, even late into the night. He, of course, didn't want to abuse her generosity. But no matter at what hour Gabriel chose to leave, his father complained that he was quitting too early. Gabriel explained that his wife was alone, but Julián paid that reason no attention. Gabriel's departures therefore became a point of conflict that he didn't quite understand, until he realized that the regularity of his visits had prompted his father to entertain thoughts of passing on his business, of Gabriel's coming in more often to help out.

Gabriel also realized that his father exhibited no curiosity about him. Whatever Gabriel did for a living, what his wife was like, whether he had fathered any children appeared of no interest to Julián. Maybe, Gabriel suspected, he himself had not been generous and had behaved overly guarded. Maybe Julián was waiting for him to open up a little.

On his next visit, as the jukebox played at its customary deafening level, Gabriel volunteered that he was studying to be an X-ray technician. His father either heard and didn't react or he didn't hear, or he simply didn't care. This indifference confused Gabriel and dissipated any enthusiasm for telling Julián about Sandra or anything of his life. In fact, he couldn't envision them together at the same dining table, with Julián talking endlessly about himself. But giving him the benefit of a doubt, Gabriel tore an empty tab slip from a pad and wrote down his phone number. Julián looked at the number and asked what it was. When Gabriel said that Julián could call him some time, his father tore up the paper, "*No llamo a nadie.* I don't call anybody."

9

Dropping off the Harley-Davidson didn't take long. Umberto, a bald, middle-aged gas station owner, who in his white *guayabera* didn't look like a bike rider, said he had taken a test ride in San Juan and left it so Julián could tune it up and deliver it. Umberto inspected the motor, gunned it several times, rode the bike around the block, then shut it off and paid in cash.

As he counted out the money, he asked with a smirk how Julián's latest hustle was coming along. Miguel took the joke in stride, answering in Spanish, "You know him, always falls like a cat." Angelina had given instructions to say nothing about Julián's death lest the gas station owner get smart and make phony claims of some understanding they had. Later, in the van, Miguel figured that Julián had wrangled nine hundred out of Tito maybe because their shrewd father had something on the guy.

"Pops, man, with him you never know. He probably got the bike for peanuts somehow. Maybe from a guy who stole it." They were on the avenue toward the highway back to San Juan. "Did anybody ever tell you about what he used to do with migrant workers, man? He used to sell them this charter deal, charge them for the flight, fly over with them, then he drove them in a bus he rented, charging them for the bus transportation, then he would get a commission from the farmers."

Before reaching the turnoff to the northbound highway, Miguel got an idea. Farther east, down the coastal road, were several seaside restaurants. Gabriel remarked that he didn't have that much cash, but Miguel grinned, patting the wad of bills in his shirt pocket. Gabriel reminded him that Angelina said that she needed to pay for the funeral expenses.

"You believe her, man? She's slick, I tell you. The brothers paid for that party. Uncle Celestino told me. She's just trying to keep what's left. This is part of our inheritance too. Pops should take us to lunch. That's right." He crossed the intersection, headed for the coastal road.

Gabriel picked out a place he had been to before, the Restaurante Vistas Azules. Except for a table with a caucus of three business types, on this late Friday afternoon the restaurant was otherwise empty. The two sat facing the Caribbean with the bright late afternoon sun to the west. Gabriel was well into his second *Cuba libre* when the broiled lobsters arrived, huge, splayed out on enormous plates. By that time Miguel had described in detail the Bonjour female cousins worth getting to know better. He was also filled in on the uncles, the extensive branchings of the family, and some dirt on the people Gabriel met at Aunt Wilma's after the burial. Miguel waxed gingerly cynical. With Julián gone, his attitude seemed to be that they were really no longer his family.

The red sun was now bleeding into its own reflection on the Caribbean. The beauty of the sunset justified their decision to have eaten there, paying with their inheritance. By the time the waiter served them their second *café con leche,* Venus was twinkling, and the room had filled with diners. When their long lunch seemed to come to an end, Miguel unexpectedly ordered brandy for the both of them. This worried Gabriel, as he thought of Miguel's drunk tantrum the day before. Reading Gabriel's mind, he immediately placated, "Don't worry, just a little brandy won't get me drunk. I'll be all right to drive."

10

On a cold, overcast fall day Gabriel and Mami Blanca left Clemencia's apartment to move into their own place, farther south in the Bronx, a second-floor walk-up that faced St. Mary's Park. The new apartment smelled of fresh paint and the furniture was new, but Mami Blanca had not yet gotten a television set. She showed him his new room, then took him to St. Luke's School, which was two blocks away, where he would continue the sixth grade. She said that she had already spoken to the principal the week before, so she just had to fill out some forms. But on that day St. Luke's was on a half-day schedule, so by the time Mami Blanca got through the registration process the classes were being let out.

They returned to the apartment with Mami Blanca urging him to hurry up because she had asked for only the morning off from work and had to prepare him lunch. She was due at work by 1:00. He asked who was going to take care of him, and she explained that, because she couldn't yet afford to pay anybody, he had to spend the afternoon alone. In fact, he would stay home alone every afternoon when he got home from school, too. Mami Blanca talked to him about being brave and ordered him to stay upstairs and not to open the door for anybody no matter who they were, even friends.

He liked the view of the park and that this apartment was sunnier than Clemencia's. He looked out on the park as he listened or half-listened to Mami Blanca's instructions and words of encouragement. She continued to speak from the bedroom as she got ready to go to work. The teachers at St. Luke's give a lot of homework, so he won't be bored all the time that he's alone. He should turn on the radio if he feels lonely. They will have a TV soon. Her number at work was taped next to the phone. He can call her once in the afternoon but no more than one time, unless it's an emergency, because her boss will get annoyed. Gabriel could smell her perfume from the living room as he noticed only a few people were walking through the gray, chilly park with leafless trees.

Just then a black car double-parked below his window. A man in a blue coat got out, opened the truck. Gabriel hollered to Mami Blanca to come, come quickly to the window. His excitement brought her briskly. Carrying a long, rectangular box lengthwise by the tight twine wrapped around it, Julián was about to enter the building. Before entering he paused to put down the box and happened to look up. Gabriel waved franticly, prompting his father to smile. In no time there was a knocking at the door. Mami Blanca aimed one eye through the peephole, then turned the three locks on the door. A savory aroma blew into the apartment, covering over the smell of new paint.

Mami Blanca reacted dryly. "*¿Cómo te enteraste que vivimos aquí?* How did you find out we live here?"

"I bumped into Clemencia last week in the garment district. She told me that you had found your own place, and when you planned to move, so I brought this to celebrate." He carried the greasy box to the dining table.

"She never mentioned anything about seeing you." Clemencia was strange that way. Gabriel, she always said, needed his father no matter how bad he was, but it was Clemencia as much as Mami Blanca who drilled into him his dislike of Julián. Every time that his mother was about to leave him with Clemencia to go out dancing with her girlfriends, Gabriel heard Clemencia remind Mami Blanca not to make the same mistake of getting attached to another skirt chaser.

Julián removed a handkerchief from his pocket and wiped grease from his hands. When he finished, he addressed Gabriel, who stared at him as if he were looking at an apparition. "Gabriel, don't you greet your father?" Gabriel flew into Julián's open arms. "You must never forget that I am your father."

"Julián, this is a very bad moment. I have to be downtown in less than an hour . . ."

"Relax, relax, I'll drive you there."

"It's in Manhattan . . ."

"I don't care if it's in China."

The aroma coming from the box was killing Gabriel, who put his hand on the box and felt heat. Julián asked Mami Blanca for a knife, but Gabriel ran into the kitchen to get it. Julián cut the twine holding the two halves of the box tight. As he proceeded to cut, he began a story of how he had received the contents as payment for a favor. Mami Blanca walked off into her bedroom, "Go on, I'm listening." He had lent this guy some money when he desperately needed it. Today that person paid back in full, and in gratitude for Julián's coming through he prepared him what was in the box. The cords cut, he lifted the top and inside was an entire shiny-crisp, still-warm, delicious-smelling roast pig.

Gabriel called out Mami Blanca to see it. She came out with her face freshly made up and her coat hanging over one shoulder. Julián looked at her a long time. In the act of putting on her coat, Blanca simply walked up to the box, looked down at the pig and said, "*Gracias.*" She went into the kitchen, took out a dish and cut some pieces with a carving knife. Before putting it away, she forbade Gabriel from cutting any more pieces with the big knife, ordering him to use the smaller one, then reminded him not to open the door for anybody, and mentioned that if he didn't want pork for lunch, in the refrigerator he would find a sandwich she had prepared and a banana, and to secure all three locks after she leaves. She gave him a kiss, opened the door and left. Julián gave Gabriel a kiss, a big hug, then rushed to catch up to her. From the window, Gabriel watched his mother hesitate but finally get talked into getting in the car and being chauffeured.

By the time Mami Blanca returned to prepare dinner, Gabriel had stuffed himself all afternoon with pork meat, pork fat and crisp pork rind. Before going to bed he asked Mami Blanca if his father was going to visit again soon. Mami Blanca didn't think so, not for a while. He was moving back to Puerto Rico.

| |

"This van doesn't want to get back, man, just like me." The missing engine chugged and choked up the incline at a pedestrian's pace. The engine's problem corrected itself then recurred as they approached the exit for the town of Barranquitas, whose name seemed important to Miguel: "Pops once took me along to see a friend, and he took us to this hick dance place around here. *Jíbara* girls, good dancing, cheap drinks. We danced our brains out, then we all went to a motel and got laid. I never forgot that night. I remember we turned off here." Speaking mainly to himself, without consulting Gabriel, he took the exit.

On the dark country road, the bright headlight beams reached into long stretches of road lined with blossoming flamboyant trees that formed tunnels with red-orange ceilings of intertwined branches. Cool black air blew into Gabriel's open window. Above the treetops shone the Caribbean's horizontally halved moon. Miguel excitedly pursued their destination, thinking out loud his reconstruction of the path, while the van, as if Miguel's excitement had made it forget its physical ailments, zipped up and down the hilly terrain. They came to the entrance of a *cafetín* where a foursome of men played dominoes under a floodlight. Miguel pulled aside, wished them a good evening, and asked them for directions, describing the place he remembered. They all pointed further down the road, about two kilometers. It was called the *Caracol,* the Seashell.

They heard the sounds of the club before seeing it at the foot of the next hill, in a wide field where a few cars were parked around it. Inside the place was dimly lit. The music they heard while parking came from a jukebox, which played while the musicians were setting up. Three customers were at the bar, tended to by two women, one a young black woman with tight pants and the other an older platinum blond in a dress. She was either chubby in the waist or pregnant. A gray-haired man in a white suit and pink shirt sat at one end of the bar. He was being chummy with a blond costumer with her back to the room. The black barmaid was very pretty and shapely with flashing bright eyes, but she was also boisterous and sloppy in her manner, constantly talking to the other barmaid with a yelling voice. When Miguel and Gabriel sat at a table, she yelled out to ask them what they wanted to drink. The man in the white suit, distracted from his conversation every time the barmaid said anything, ordered her to shut up that mouth.

Miguel, recalling that night he was last at the Caracol, when Julián's friend kept ordering rounds of whiskey and coconut milk, insisted that they too should drink whiskey and coconut milk. That friend, whose name Miguel forgot, was really also there to hook up with a woman that he'd been seeing on the sneak. He lived in San Juan, so nobody knew his face around those parts. His girlfriend arrived with a blond woman friend whom Julián seemed to know pretty well. There was also a third woman, who immediately became Miguel's date. Later he found out that Julián had paid her to join them. The following day was Miguel's eighteenth birthday, and that woman was Julián's gift. She was in her twenties and, Miguel said stroking his paunch, he was thin back then and a not bad-looking young tiger who got his decent share, so he didn't perceive this woman's being paid to be with him as a slight. At first he worried that the girl, who was a brunette, would reject him for his color. Luckily, that problem didn't come up because his hooker date performed flirtatiously and really seemed to be enjoying herself. But he needed several drinks to really get into the night's fun and stop himself from looking over at Julián and his blond honey.

He had never before seen his father's charmer side go to work on a woman. She had firm wide hips and full legs and wore very high heels. She looked really hot, like an actress, with big eyes and a stare that seemed to hypnotize Julián, whose face became milder-looking than Miguel had ever seen it. At some point Julián apparently said something endearing to her, and she melted all over, putting her hand to his cheek, pressing her cheek to his, then wrapping her palm around the nape of his neck as they danced.

Miguel's date, whose name he forgot, reacted to his all-consuming attention to that other woman, never imagining that he was actually jealous of that blond for extracting such tenderness from Julián. He thought briefly about his mother, but this being the only time he felt close to his father, he pushed that guilt aside. Besides, he couldn't think straight, having watched Julián with that blond piece of ass while the hooker worked harder to get his full concentration, gently stroking his neck with her hand. Miguel's story had no real ending except his sliding into a gloomy introspection.

After a brief lull, Miguel motioned to the waitress, who didn't notice him. Miguel's having emptied his first drink in a couple of swigs as he told his story prompted Gabriel to sip his drink very slowly so his glass was still half-full. He asked Miguel not to order more for him, hoping that Miguel would take this request as a subtle way of asking him not to drink anymore. But Miguel either didn't hear or didn't listen and, catching the waitress' eye, gave a circular hand signal.

Gabriel looked around. In the course of Miguel's story, the previously empty tables filled up with couples and groups from all ages, from teenagers to seniors. The older patrons hadn't waited for the live band and had already set the mood by dancing to the vintage *plenas* playing on the jukebox. Now the live band was playing, and customers overflowed out the three open doors, and many stood in the field, drinks in hand, coming in just to dance. Dancing being foremost on everybody's agenda, the generations freely mixed and matched: the younger women were taken first, by both young and older men, but what older women were available inevitably danced too, with the first men to ask, some old, some young.

Gabriel surveyed the available women. Miguel, now well into his fourth drink, encouraged him to put a smile on his face and get out there because he himself was ready. Behind Miguel's shoulder, over at the bar the blond who had been talking with the owner had turned to face the room. She seemed well preserved, and their eyes briefly met. Her look was straight, without flinching. He turned away, seeking out a younger woman for a partner, but none was available. At the end of the last dance, Miguel's eyes followed a chubby cinnamon-colored woman, who returned from the floor to her table.

She was seated among a group of black women sitting directly behind him. When the band started up again, Miguel smoothly pirouetted on his chair and requested the next dance of that chubby woman. She acquiesced with a smile, taking his hand. Miguel then leaned over and said something to his partner's friend, a younger woman with a generous smile and short hair combed tightly back, who stood up. Miguel took her hand and led her to Gabriel, who found himself coerced by chivalry to dance.

She was rail thin and felt delicate in Gabriel's arms. Her smooth, deep chocolate complexion warmed his cheek. She danced fluidly but modestly, making certain their bodies did not touch. After a few turns of this *plena,* Gabriel asked her name. Her friends called her

Nila. As he told her his name and where he was from, behind her passed the blond from the bar, who was dancing with a shorter, gray-haired man. A seasoned *plena* dancer, he had some fancy moves, and the woman kept up with him. As she moved rhythmically with him, he noted her plump figure in a pink dress, her large hips and full legs, her diminutive feet perched on high heels. Amidst his circular moves with Nila, Gabriel and the blond came almost face-to-face, and she delivered the briefest, almost indiscernible smile. Gabriel completed his dance with Nila, and met Miguel at their table.

"Fine woman, gentle," Miguel praised his partner, then started a dissertation on the kind of women he liked, to which Gabriel paid no attention, distracted by the blond woman at the bar. He also didn't hear Miguel order another round for them and for the women at Nila's table. The extra drink that Gabriel had not yet touched was also now on Miguel's side of the table and almost empty. Miguel lifted his glass as if to toast their finding this place. "That night was probably the closest I'd ever been with Pops, man."

The band started another dance, a cheek-to-cheek *bolero* this time, but Miguel didn't move. His mood had suddenly changed. Behind him, some young lion had swooped down to take Nila out on the dance floor, but Gabriel didn't have plans to dance anyway, distracted by Miguel's mood shift. He waved off Gabriel's question if everything was okay. "Grab somebody's hand and dance, man, don't sit there looking at me."

Turning away, Gabriel's sight connected with the eyes of the blond woman by the bar. Taking Miguel's advice, he went over to her. She simply accepted his hand. Close up, she looked older than she appeared from a distance in dim light, old enough to be his mother. But he was glad to be dancing with her although beyond this desire to dance with her, he didn't know what to do with her, what to say to her. Julián denied him his gene for that talent.

At first he thought he would simply dance and thank her and leave things as they were, but words blurted out. He asked to know her name. It was Doris. He introduced himself. She asked him why she hadn't seen him at the Caracol before. His longer sentences in crappy Spanish confirmed the obvious reason. "*Veo. No eres de aquí.* I see.

You're not from here." He nodded, explaining that he was visiting from New York. While answering her, he remembered why he had flown down. Julián's funeral had taken place years ago in his memory.

"I'm from nearby. I used to come here often a long time ago. The Caracol used to be called something else. It has been here . . . well, a while. I am a widow, but I only go out every now and then."

Gabriel got lost in her large eyes. She was once a stunner. He must have said more than he realized with his stare because she re-acted by putting her hand on his cheek, sliding it slowly to the back of his neck. This gesture sent sexual shock waves through Gabriel. For a timeless interval, he danced oblivious to everything but the music and the rhythm of her body against his, a pleasure interrupted when he noticed that Miguel, who had apparently shaken off his bad mood and was now dancing with his chubby partner again, stared at them strangely as he swirled around them. When Miguel floated out of his sight, Gabriel returned to his enjoyment of the music and Doris.

He was immersed completely in this pleasure when he heard shouting and noticed that the entire room looked in the direction of the commotion. The cinnamon woman that Miguel had been dancing with ran away from him, and Miguel raised his hand and pointed toward her, "Fuck you, you bitch." Oblivious to the sur-rounding reaction of the dancers, who had cleared wide around him, Miguel returned to his table cursing in English in his lion's roar. He seemed not to notice that men were closing in from differ-ent angles of the room. The first one who reached him said some-thing that made Miguel get louder, telling him to "Fuck off." The man's date and others around him stopped his fist from reaching Miguel. Doris whispered in Gabriel's ear, "*Sácalo de aquí.* Get him out of here."

But Gabriel knew there was no grabbing him or reasoning. He went over to Miguel, and in his broken Spanish to placate the men, he explained that his *"amigo"* was grieving over a loss. But the men just wanted him to reap the personal satisfaction of teaching him a lesson in behavior. Then, accompanied by the man in the white suit,

Doris stepped in. Immediately respected by the angry men, she was able to persuade them to let the two leave unharmed.

The owner signaled to the band to play. But, as if he had nothing to do with the entire affair, Miguel sat defiantly, in a world of his own, drowned out by the band when he repeated to himself that nobody should fuck with him. Gabriel whispered into his ear, "Little brother, it's time to go."

"You're right!" He rose and swaggered out. Gabriel thanked Doris, holding her hand, divided as part of him wished he could dawdle in this sexual fantasy while another part wanted to be gone completely from the entire experience. Doris urged him to catch up to Miguel before somebody pounced on him outside.

When they reached the van, Miguel surrendered the keys without resistance. He said practically nothing as the van growled up and down hilly dark roads. Gabriel preferred to remain ignorant of what had happened back there than to stir up Miguel's passions. He mused instead on his own hurried departure from Doris, his shaking her hand and dashing out, practically escaping because he didn't understand his attraction to her and he wouldn't have known where to take things.

Every so many miles, Miguel grumbled something. He nodded off for stretches. Twice he asked if they had reached San Juan. Just before entering the city, he woke up, ordered Gabriel to pull over and stop, whereupon he opened his door, jumped out and puked. Reeking but calmer, he came back into the van, found the pint bottle and washed out his mouth with rum. "I want to get the fuck out of here."

At the circular turn off to different metropolitan sections, Miguel made roaringly plain what he meant, "No, man, go right, take me to the fucking airport." He tugged at the wheel so the van swerved menacingly, causing cars in the right lane to screech to a halt. Gabriel pulled over to the shoulder, "Maybe you should think this over. You were drinking a lot, and . . ."

"I don't want to hear your white boy, big brother bullshit. Take me to the fucking airport or let me drive."

12

. . . Gabriel drove up to the main terminal. Miguel could have
caught a last flight to anywhere, or he could be sprawled out over
a row of chairs. As there was no policeman or traffic at that hour,
Gabriel left the van at the curb and wandered into the desolate terminal waiting area. According to the monitors, all the late flights to
southern states had gone out on time. He went to the security gate
through which Miguel must have passed. A uniformed woman and
man stood by the scanners. They told him that a large black man
had gone by in a hurry, but that he certainly must have boarded the
last flight out, which was to Miami, because he hadn't come back.
No one was permitted to spend the night at the gate. The security
group itself was only there waiting for a storm delay from Boston.
Miguel, it would appear, had taken off.

Gabriel was undecided whether to drive to Lucy's and return the
van in the morning or pass by Angelina's and drop off the van, then
take a cab home. Sooner or later, he had to explain that Miguel had
skipped out with her money. What he really wanted was to make a
run for it, like Miguel, just disappear from the Bonjours and Puerto
Rico, but Angelina might deduce that they had both conspired to
divide her money. She would disturb his aunts by going to Lucy's to
find out what had happened to the money, so this headache would
only boomerang. Angelina must have already called his aunts to find
out if they had heard from Miguel and Gabriel. There was no way
out: his destiny was to be the courier of Miguel's act of revenge
against Julián. He would return to Angelina's that night, put an end
to the episode, then start afresh the following morning and the rest
of his life.

On the way to Angelina's, he wondered if he will ever again see
Miguel, at once his brother and an angry stranger in whose presence
he felt like vinegar poured on a open wound. Gabriel's being the spit-
ting image of Julián seemed to preclude any reconciliation and make
their seeing each other again unlikely. This separation was probably
what Julián wanted because, Gabriel realized just then, his father
surely lived ashamed that in the untraceable shuffle of Bonjour

genes, Miguel might also be the dark brown fruit of his own blood. Gabriel caught a glimpse of his face in the rearview mirror, recalling Julián's tawnier complexion. Poor Miguel had paid dearly so their father could punish himself, Gabriel thought, an epiphany that left him speechless, in a mental vacuum.

On turning the corner to Angelina's street, the thought of Angie immediately filled the vacuum. All that day he had struggled to suppress any thoughts of her. When he finally parked in front of Angelina's building, her daughter seemed to be the real underlying reason why he had decided to come. He looked at his watch. It was past 1 A.M., maybe too late for anyone to be up. From the sidewalk he could see that the living room glowed with the light of a television screen.

Before pressing the buzzer to the building, he paused to prepare himself for the possible consequences of this walk up three flights. He was married, he reminded himself, and Sandra surely deserved better than the tempest that his nascent feelings toward Angie might rain down on his marriage. And he hadn't called Sandra in two days. On the other hand, Angie hadn't expressed any interest in him, so his visit might simply prove insignificant, brotherly. Besides, there was no avoiding that Angelina had to be told what happened to Miguel and her money.

That final argument was the weaker one, as a phone call would have served, but he was standing right at Angelina's gate, and if he willed on himself a stern discipline before the sight of Angie then nothing wrong will happen. He would simply deliver the bad news about Miguel and leave. He pressed the buzzer button. Angelina appeared silhouetted in the dark balcony and threw down the key to the gate.

She hadn't been able to sleep and was waiting to hear from him and Miguel. Her eyes were red. Gabriel sat in Julián's favorite chair and reported that Miguel had grabbed a flight to somewhere, probably Miami. As he spoke, Angie came out wearing a royal blue robe, her black hair loose. She switched on the lamp, turned off the already muted television set, then sat beside her mother on the sofa.

Caught off guard by her coming into the room, Gabriel stumbled as he related a carefully selected sequence of the day's events although apparently sounding unconvincing because Angelina, as if sensing he had shortchanged her of key details, kept asking him to repeat some things. Gabriel in fact had told of the dinner at her expense, skirting the dance club episode completely, but his account was generally true: Miguel insisted they stop for drinks and then he became irrational and violent, behaving in a way consistent with the first time that Gabriel met him. When Angelina finally stopped asking questions, her mood had already changed. "Well, I had to give him the fare home anyway. He deserves the few dollars left over. Julián made him suffer enough and left him nothing."

Gabriel listened to her, struggling to keep from staring at Angie's blackest eyes. Her milk-smooth skin, her almost blue hair, that mouth as if pouting combined to mesmerize him, invoking Julián's spirit to enter his body and again lose his mind over this young version of Angelina.

He stood up and asked Angelina if she minded that he take the van to drive back to his aunts' house. But Angelina would not hear of Julián's son leaving so late to drive around in the dangerous city. He assured her that he didn't mind driving late, and besides he had to call his wife.

Angelina begged him to grant her this favor: Julián's dream had always been that Gabriel would come down to the island and stay with him. As she expressed this wish, her eyes got red again. "Call your wife, let her know that everything is okay. Tomorrow morning you can eat breakfast with us and Angie can drive you, to your aunts or wherever you want."

Angie consented with silence, averting his eyes by rolling hers in the direction of the balcony. The prospect of a day with her overtook him. He remained of two minds, even as his Bonjour body descended into Julián's chair.

Jacobo Timerman
Prisoner without a Name, Cell without a Number

David Unger
Life in the Damn Tropics: A Novel